Camilla's Roses

Also by Bernice L. McFadden
in Large Print:

Sugar
This Bitter Earth
The Warmest December
Loving Donovan

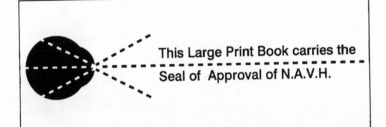

This Large Print Book carries the
Seal of Approval of N.A.V.H.

Camilla's Roses

Bernice L. McFadden

Thorndike Press • Waterville, Maine

Published in 2004 by arrangement with Dutton, a member of Penguin Group (USA) Inc.

Thorndike Press® Large Print African-American.

The tree indicium is a trademark of Thorndike Press.

The text of this Large Print edition is unabridged. Other aspects of the book may vary from the original edition.

Set in 16 pt. Plantin by Al Chase.

Printed in the United States on permanent paper.

Library of Congress Cataloging-in-Publication Data

McFadden, Bernice L.
    Camilla's roses / Bernice L. McFadden.
      p. cm.
    ISBN 0-7862-6792-5 (lg. print : hc : alk. paper)
    1. Breast — Cancer — Patients — Fiction.   2. Parent and adult child — Fiction.   3. Mothers and daughters — Fiction.   4. Cancer in women — Fiction.   5. Large type books.   I. Title.
PS3563.C3622C36 2004
813'.54—dc22
                                      2004047394

For the Circle:

Andrea, CeCe, Dawn, Daisy, Gloria,
Darice and Lauretta,
And my family,
For them all.

As the Founder/CEO of NAVH, the only national health agency solely devoted to those who, although not totally blind, have an eye disease which could lead to serious visual impairment, I am pleased to recognize Thorndike Press★ as one of the leading publishers in the large print field.

Founded in 1954 in San Francisco to prepare large print textbooks for partially seeing children, NAVH became the pioneer and standard setting agency in the preparation of large type.

Today, those publishers who meet our standards carry the prestigious "Seal of Approval" indicating high quality large print. We are delighted that Thorndike Press is one of the publishers whose titles meet these standards. We are also pleased to recognize the significant contribution Thorndike Press is making in this important and growing field.

Lorraine H. Marchi, L.H.D.
Founder/CEO
NAVH

★ Thorndike Press encompasses the following imprints: Thorndike, Wheeler, Walker and Large Print Press

New lives begin with a question.
Do you love me? Will you marry me? Will you have my child?
Some people think it's in the telling, but I know it's in the asking.

Rose

Charlottesville, unable to claim Georgia or Florida, but settling in both places; its name in place, but state allegiance caught up in red tape and government paperwork until the latter part of the eighteenth century when the town was divided into Charlottesville (on Georgia land) and Charlotte Bay (on the Florida side).

But the people that called the town home had known the place for so long just as Charlottesville that they found it hard to refer to it as anything else. The return addresses found on letters that were sent to family and friends that relocated to different parts of the country stated: who and what street, road or route and then just, Charlottesville, USA.

A quaint town, filled with people who lived in harmony; tiny wooden houses, barns well-stocked with grain; preserves in the cellar, animals fat and content.

Abundant in everything anyone could ever want.

Charlottesville was dense with vegeta-

tion brought over during slavery times. Java plum and carob trees dotted the countryside, jungle berry bushes climbed trestles and wood fences and there was an abundance of strawberry guava trees at the mouth of town.

All of those exotic plants, trees, and shrubs were commonplace in Charlottesville, found in any backyard or the wide yawn of land that wouldn't be developed until the mid-1950s.

It was as unique a place as it was common; boasting nine-month-long summers and residents that had only heard of snow.

Hope was everywhere in that small place few had heard of; resting in the dawn of each new day, in the blue jays' song and seen in the young eyes of the laughing children that played tag around the massive barks of the African tulip trees.

Almost perfect.

It was the rosebush that caused the envy and thievery.

Where it came from, no one knew for sure. Algiers or Morocco, depending on who was telling the story.

One of a kind and thriving on Hurston land is what caused the problems.

Horticulturists came from all over the

country to see this rosebush that did not grow in any other part of the country and all of the attention elevated its owners up to a kind of celebrity status.

It had been stolen a number of times, dug up in the thick of night and hauled away by some jealous neighbor, but always returned, wilted and half-dead.

"Heathens," Abbey said as she steadied the bush in place as Joseph shoveled dirt back into the hole and patted it into place.

Back in its own soil, in its front-yard home again, the rosebush flourished and so did Abbey, coming up pregnant each time the rosebush was stolen and returned; she gave birth to ten children; eight girls and two boys, christening every one of the girls with the middle name Rose. And they in turn did the same and the same holds true for every girl child after that and so on and so on.

Years later the tradition still holds firm and continues in that place that claims two states, with no zip code and one rosebush, but it also flourishes in a borough named after a little-known English royal that is bordered by the sea, where remnants of a world's fair still stands; it still thrives in a place called Queens.

The Present

Camilla Rose

Tuesday was their day.

Camilla picked out a matching thong and demi-cup bra. Purple-and-black mesh that showed most everything.

She sat down at her dressing table and admired herself in the mirror as she squirted on some perfume, plucked at a few stray eyebrow hairs that had burrowed through since her last waxing.

The car pulled into the driveway and then the front door opened. There were greetings exchanged between employer and employee and then the heavy sigh her husband Bryant always took before he began to climb their sweeping staircase.

When he walked into the bedroom she was seated on the mahogany four-poster king-sized bed, facing him, bent over seductively so that her hair covered her eyes. She had on the spiked black pumps she'd bought for an art reception they'd attended some time back, the pumps he said did something to her legs, something that drove him wild. She remembered he couldn't stop staring at her that night, those pumps, that dress, and the way she wore her hair swept up, except for a few strands that floated down her neck, bouncing and beckoning him to kiss her shoulder blades. Which he did, every time he called for another martini.

He told her, on the way home that night, that she'd have to keep them on, the pumps, and when he got her home that night he fucked her until she thought he'd break himself off inside of her.

Now, sitting there on the bed, her legs spread wide, the mesh material barely covering her vaginal lips, and throwing even more coals onto the fire by twirling a lollipop between her candy-apple red–painted lips.

Bryant dropped his briefcase and pushed the door shut behind him.

"Crawl," she said and Bryant plummeted to his knees and did just that.

Tuesday was their day.

It was after that and the lovemaking and the soft talk before the quiet of resting in each other's arms and Lena, the housekeeper, tapping on their bedroom door and whispering that she would look after their daughter, Zola, until they came down for dinner.

It was after all that that Bryant stepped in behind her in the shower, kissed her neck, and cupped her soapy breasts in his hands and caressed her still-erect nipples between his forefinger and thumb and then pressed his hard-again penis against her backside and allowed his passion to carry him away and squeezed her breast a little too roughly for Camilla's liking, even though she didn't voice her protest, it wasn't until then that he felt the lump.

"What's this?"

"What's this?" That question took on a life of its own, Bryant's textured tone dropping away, not even the letters of that question remained. When she heard it reverberating in her ears, she could not picture the spelling of the words. That question became the sound of an angry ocean, the color of slate, the question mark itself, a dagger.

She couldn't get a mammogram until the following Monday and that lump seemed to grow with every dawning day. She couldn't keep her hands off of it. She pushed and prodded, rubbed and pinched it. But it wouldn't go away. She pressed hot compresses against it and then ice packs. She rubbed salve on it and the green pulp from

17

the aloe vera plant. She cupped it at night and spoke to it, prayed it away, and cursed it to hell.

Bryant told her she was worried about nothing. Babette, her mother-in-law, said that it was probably just a cyst. A cyst. And besides, "You're just thirty years old for chrissakes. You're too young for it to be anything but a cyst," she said.

The easiest thing to do would be to pretend like there had been no discovery in the shower, no phone call to Dr. Franklin, and no Monday. Camilla was good at pretending things away.

But she found this situation to be a bit more challenging. The lump was a daily nuisance and the word *Monday* mocked her from her wall and desk calendars. Only the phone call could be dismissed as fantasy.

The week inched by and Camilla busied herself with work, giving her best advice on lazy husbands, wayward children, and vindictive girlfriends.

The letter that had asked her if she was Camilla Rose from 142nd Avenue, she destroyed that in the paper shredder — and a minute later when she looked at the spaghetti-thin strips splayed at the bottom of the bin, she pretended that it was bank correspondence offering her yet another low-interest, high-credit, charge card.

The days eke by until Monday is upon her and she finds herself sitting in the waiting room, dressed in a Gap T-shirt and denim capris, studying the copper polish on her toenails, coaxing her mind to think of pleasantries: sunflowers, white roses, and the first time she and Poe kissed. That last thought had surprised her and her head snapped up as if she had blurted the thought out loud.

"Camilla Boston?"

Her name is called and some of the other women, who wait, glance at her pedicured feet, they watch the swing in her hips and think they hear Duke Ellington's "Take the 'A' Train," while their eyes travel up her leg scaling her curved hip, finally coming to rest in her waistline and they "humph" to themselves and straighten their backs, while making a mental note about their toes and wondering where their walking music has gone off to.

The room is made up of sterile whites and sanitary steel grays.

Camilla tries to shut out the cold gel the technician swathed across her breast, but that was hard, the technician's gloved hand, the squeeze bottle of thick white gel, the woman's smile, and her rest-assured manner, did nothing for Camilla's nerves. She could feel her buttocks clapping together, her knees beginning to quake, and the sound of her teeth chattering away in her mouth.

Poe came to mind again and the childhood nights on the patio with her cousins, all of them lying on their backs staring up at the moon, mouths crammed tight with Oreos, fireflies blinking in pickle jars.

"I know it's cold. It'll be just a moment. You'll see, you blink your eye and it'll be all over with," the technician said and lifted one of Camilla's heavy breasts and set it on top of the metal shelf. She handled her breast expertly, delicately, but Camilla still felt like a piece of meat. "It'll pinch," the technician said before she walked over to the control panel and pressed the button.

The top shelf came down and squashed Camilla's left breast. She felt tears stinging at the corner of her eyes. Velma had pinched her many times. Camilla knew what a pinch felt like, this was something else.

"That wasn't so bad, was it?" the technician said and readied Camilla's right breast.

Later, for the sonogram, Camilla lies on

the table in a dark room while technician number two rolls the sensor across her left breast and then the right. It was the same procedure she'd had done when she was pregnant with Zola. But this time she wasn't watching the screen for a hand, a foot, and sweet lips sucking happily on a thumb.

This time she strained to see the mass. And sure enough, there it was.

Dr. Franklin chewed on his bottom lip as he examined the X rays. He scratched at his chin and made a sound in his throat before giving his full attention to Camilla.

"Well, Camilla, it seems as though there is something here. In both breasts. Something small," he said and used his thumb and forefinger to imitate just how small. "But to be sure, we should take a biopsy. Just a precautionary measure. Nothing to be concerned about."

Camilla nodded her head and heard her mother-in-law in her mind: Milk duct. Cyst.

But then the question came.

"Camilla, let me ask you this, do you have a history of cancer in your family?"

What family?

Camilla was a phoenix who rose from the

rubble, a ghost who appeared out of the blue.

Dr. Franklin was a family friend and had been present and smiling at the engagement party. He had heard the story of how she and Bryant came to be a couple and when he looked around and saw that he knew practically everybody there, he swirled the ice around in his crystal glass filled with Wild Turkey and asked, "Where are your people, Camilla?"

A hush seemed to descend on them and Babette gave Dr. Franklin a tight smile, hooked him by his elbow and guided him back toward the bar. "Come, Cedric, I think your drink needs topping off."

Whatever Babette told him seemed to be satisfying because he never broached the subject again although Camilla had the feeling that despite Babette's words he wanted to ask her even as he slouched in the sixth pew of the glass cathedral church.

She saw him, Dr. Franklin, wheezing beneath the sixty extra pounds he'd piled on after his hip surgery, mopping his forehead with a blue handkerchief and twisting his head this way and that in order to try to get the best view he could from behind Odessa Harris and her Empire State Building–high hat that had a brim as wide as wings, ruining the view for Dr. Franklin and guests ten rows deep.

She had the feeling he wanted to ask her right then in front of God and Bryant's family and friends and her heart had beat extra fast when the minister got to the, "Does anyone have any objections why this man and this woman should . . ."

He knew her story. Not the real one, of course. No one knew the truth.

Now Camilla suspected that the question he posed was just another way at getting at the truth.

She blinked at him, hoping the very gesture would erase his question and take with it the memory of those people and that house pressed into the corner of Foch Boulevard and 142nd Avenue. That house, whitewashed and trimmed in gray, with a black-shingled roof that pointed and then sloped.

Four bedrooms and a rickety staircase that climbed past the stained-glass window that had been broken a number of times over the years, but never replaced, just patched with masking tape and the thin sheets of plastic that her grandmother, Velma, saved whenever she picked up some article of clothing from the dry cleaner.

Living room, dining room and good-sized

kitchen that led out to a small porch and then down to the backyard.

That house sprouted children, seemed to grow grown folks; aunts that came to visit for a spell, the ones that dropped consonants from their words, cussed when they felt like it, talked with their mouths full, made no apologies for who they were; goddamn it, they had made it through — through wilds of Africa, slavery, emancipation, reconstruction, segregation, and the thirty-two-hour bus ride here!

They called it as they saw it and referred to most everybody as *baby* — sucked marrow from chicken bones, licked their fingers clean after a meal, scratched where it itched no matter who was watching, laughed openmouthed, and passed out kisses and hard candy just because some little one was so damn cute.

The uncles, necks scented with Old Spice or Aqua Velva, they chew tobacco, some roll their own cigarettes. Coffee in the morning and whiskey in the afternoon through evening. Always sipping on something and uttering "Jesus" at least three times a day.

Morning time, their eyes still crusted with sleep and breath rank as they slide, slip, and ease their way across the sheets and press themselves into their still-sleeping spouses, dicks hard and poking, hands tugging and pulling until the women stop slapping and the "uh-uh" and "git now!" turns into silky moans and legs part and the women flower right there on the sheets.

Afternoon time and the men are uttering it again; walking down the street, tossing dice against a brick wall or talking shit in the barbershop all the time watching the young things bounce by. Miniskirts, platform shoes. All to die for. "Jesus," the men whisper and rub the inside of their thighs.

Later in the evening, kids put down for the night, a game of spades, tonk, or dominoes going on at the dining room table; the women close by, seated at the elbows of their men or milling about in the kitchen, whispering, giggling, brushing crumbs off of the counter, pulling back the shade to check on the night sky. The men, one eye on the game and the other on the women, are suddenly struck speechless. Toothpicks roll across pink tongues, hearts beat soundless through the blessed moment of silence.

The men know that black women are *women* at the very least; magical at their zenith and biblical at the core, being with a black woman was as sacred as dousing oneself in holy water.

That house, square-windowed eyes, dark cousins for pupils watching the citified people with wonder and in the late summer of 1952 Camilla Rose was not even a notion; Maggie Rose held center stage in that house, even though her sister Velma Rose, still hated her and had only recently stopped wishing her dead.

The Past

Maggie Rose

She hadn't always been that way. She'd been beautiful once, practically perfect, except for the scrape on her knee and the one she got on a jutting nail when she was eight years old. But no one ever really counted that one because it was set deep inside her dimple, hidden away, almost invisible, unless you looked real close.

Caramel colored and bathed in light, nobody looked real close at Maggie; their eyes got ambushed in her long eyelashes, perfectly shaped nose and those lips, heart-shaped and a natural shade of blush. People didn't want to look at Maggie up close; it would have been too much for them, like eating sugar right from the bowl or sucking sap straight from the tree. You had to stand back to admire her, like one would do an exceptional piece of artwork.

Maggie was indeed extraordinarily beautiful but not extremely bright. She got mixed up adding one and one, couldn't spell to save her life and wore shoes without laces until she was ten years old because she just couldn't get the gist of knotting two pieces of string together.

Maggie, nineteen and still fond of dolls, playing pretend, and dress-up, not interested in boys, well, not really, preferring to stay up under her mother, baking and sewing, spending Saturday nights sitting at her father's feet, listening to him read from the Bible, watching him puff on his pipe.

Nineteen and happy just to be alive and well and big sister to Velma, just fourteen months younger than her, but not as pretty — well, not even close — but not ugly either.

Velma's got a sharp tongue and a quick temper. Angry, the townspeople say, because she inherited her father's bucket nose, but she should be grateful, they whispered, because as dark as she was, she wasn't blue-black like her daddy, because a blue-black woman would never get a husband in Charlottesville, maybe somewhere yonder, but not here, they said.

Maggie dotes on Velma, bucket nose, dark skin, ornery disposition and all. She bakes cakes for her, sews dresses from material she buys on discount from the odds-and-ends store she works at, and stands proudly at the door on Friday nights when Velma's boyfriend Lloyd George comes to collect her to go out dancing or just to town for ice cream floats.

They share a room, Maggie and Velma, and a double-sized bed that's draped with colorful quilts that Maggie has stitched together with her own beautiful hands, they snuggle together in that bed and Velma whispers secrets in Maggie's ear, confides in her about the butterflies in her stomach and the song her heart belts out every time she's close to Lloyd.

"Y'all think you gonna get married?" Maggie's voice is filled with excitement and wonder.

"Hope so," Velma says; her head already filled with baby's breath and the white-lace gloves that were wrapped in tissue and tucked away in the bottom drawer of her mother's bureau. "Lord, I hope so," she breathes and wraps her arms around Maggie's neck.

"And then the babies will come and I can go collect them from the collard-green patch out back."

Velma laughs at Maggie's ignorance. She's told her a million times where babies come from but Maggie never seems to remember that. "That's what grown folks tell little children. That ain't really where babies come from. They grow up inside of you and then come out down here." Velma had spread her legs and pointed down between them. She'd even pulled the lips far enough apart so that Maggie could see her "bell" and the hole beneath it. "This here is where the babies come out."

Maggie had just blushed and turned her head away. "Oh, you just funnin' with me."

Another time, after a spring rain, Velma had dragged her to the back porch where their cat Sweetie was mewing loudly. "Sound like a baby crying," Maggie muttered as Velma dragged her down the slick back steps. "What's the rush?" she said only after she slipped and ended up on the last step, behind first.

"Look here," Velma said and pointed to the dark space underneath the stairway. Maggie strained and stretched her neck. There was Sweetie, pushing out the third kitten of the eight she would give birth to. Maggie watched in amazement as the birth sack squeezed out of Sweetie. It looked like bubble gum to Maggie. Not the pink one, but the red one that left her tongue on fire.

"Oh my lord!" Maggie screamed. "Sweetie's gonna die! Her insides are coming out!"

Velma grabbed Maggie roughly by the shoulders. "Maggie, Sweetie is giving birth.

This is how animals are born. This is how humans are born."

Maggie had just blinked at her.

"We just like the animals. The cows, sheep, goat —"

"Cats?" Maggie had ventured.

"Uh-huh," Velma said.

Maggie hadn't always been that way; mangled and mean, but after what went on between them Velma had wished ugliness on her a million times and on the real bad days, death.

It seemed like one day Lloyd was hers and the next day he belonged to Maggie. He had tricked Maggie, Velma was sure of it, but she could only hate one of them and so that would have to be Maggie, because she was beautiful, stupid, and kind.

She'd found them in the root cellar, amongst the jars of preserves, a blanket on the floor beneath them. They were already done by the time Velma came down the stairs. She smelled them first, the stink of sex mixed up with the scent of tobacco leaves Papa had first dipped in cognac and then strung up to dry.

It was that smoky aroma that Velma spent days trying to wash out of her hair. She'd scrubbed her skin raw, trying to rid her body of the scent of them. "It was as if," she whispered to the wind one day, "their bodies had come together and caught fire."

Maggie was sitting up, her knees pulled close to her chest, hiding her naked breast. Her face was tilted upwards and bathed in the sunlight that streamed through the small window.

Lloyd was on his back, his body stretched out long. His color had gone from red to bronze over the summer, and his skin just seemed to shimmer.

His right arm bent beneath his head, the fingers on his free hand sweeping Maggie's spine, cutting through the film of perspiration there. Velma could tell even then, by the way he touched Maggie that he loved her. He had never touched Velma that way.

"What?"

That's all she could find in herself to say and Lloyd shot straight up at the sound of her voice, grabbing at the corner of the blanket, trying to hide his nakedness and what he had done.

Maggie, poor stupid beautiful Maggie, had just turned her head towards her, smiled and said "Hi, Velma."

Hi, Velma?

How stupid she was. Not understanding that Lloyd was hers and that no, it wasn't okay to do what she'd done with him. "But why?" Maggie had whined days later when Velma still wouldn't talk to her. "You said we were like Sweetie, like the animals."

Velma had gone crying to her parents about what Lloyd and Maggie had done to each other down in the root cellar. Chappo had pinched her lips together and looked to her husband for a word.

Handy lit his pipe, picked up his Bible, and invited Lloyd out to the back porch. "Don't hurt him, Papa." Velma had thrown a miserable plea at her father's back.

Unable to look at Maggie, Chappo searched the kitchen for something to do.

"But I —" Maggie didn't understand what it was she'd done wrong. "Hush now." Chappo cut her off without glancing her way.

Yes, Velma had said that and had reiterated it time and time again when she pointed out that Jeremiah Johnson had two bulls and twenty cows, their own chicken coop had just one cock, and "Look here, Maggie. Says here in the paper that they puttin' Oasis, the sable-colored thoroughbred and two-time winner of the blue ribbon, out to stud."

What else was Maggie to think about sex? Love was one thing, the Bible said you were supposed to love all of God's creatures and that's what Maggie did. Sex was something else, something her parents never spoke on, something she had come to understand from Velma.

They were, as Velma had indicated, just like the animals, so what she and Lloyd had done was okay.

Wasn't it?

Velma stood across the room, staring Maggie down, slaying her slowly with her eyes.

An hour later, a sudden wind picking up, and the voices of the men no longer sounding like the low rumble of an approaching summer storm, but crisp, like autumn. There is even laughter, and a friendly pat on Lloyd's back as they step in from the porch.

The screen door slams shut and Lloyd doesn't even look Velma's way, his eyes are all over Maggie who's too stupid to appreciate the significance.

"Well, we gone have us a weddin'," Handy announces.

Chappo waits for the rest, her face remains serene, her eyes fixed on her husband's. Velma's heart pounds in her chest.

"Since these two jumped the gun, they gonna have to tie the knot. She spoiled and I don't know one good man who'd want a spoiled woman."

Velma's mouth dropped open and then snapped shut. She was spoiled! Goddamit he had spoiled her too, her and a few other women in Charlottesville!

Maggie still didn't understand what was happening.

"Will you marry me, Maggie?" Lloyd said and then dropped down awkwardly on one knee. "I loves you, Maggie."

Velma's sight was leaving her. She was going blind with madness. Her heart jumped up and into her throat. She couldn't believe what she was hearing, what she was seeing.

"Is that what you want, Maggie?" Chappo said.

Handy had had his say and she had been patient about waiting for him to talk first, but she wasn't sending none of her daughters down the aisle, spoiled or not, if that's not what they wanted to do.

Handy's shoulders dropped some, he could feel the tail of his manhood searching frantically for a hiding space.

" 'Cause if you don't want to, you don't have to." Chappo's words were so powerful; Velma thought that it must be a written law somewhere.

Maggie looked down into Lloyd's face.

"Can we have kittens and puppies?"

"Yes, yes," Lloyd said.

Oh, my god! Velma heard her heart scream inside of her chest. She looked around wildly and her eyes settled on the ceramic mixing bowl that sat on the shelf over the sink.

"What do you think, Mama, should I?" Maggie looked to Chappo.

"It's up to you, baby."

"Papa, you think I should."

"Y—"

"It's your decision, baby." Chappo cut Handy off before he could answer. Handy's tail found the perfect hideout and settled itself between his legs.

"Velma, you think I should?"

Chappo cleared her throat, forced a smile and reached a hand out to touch Velma's trembling wrist. "Uhm, your sister is not feeling like giving out any advice now, baby," Chappo said and turned and reached for the mixing bowl. "Git yourself together, girl," she hissed at Velma. "My mama gave me this bowl."

"Well, I guess it'll be okay as long as I can have a puppy and a kitten," Maggie said and Velma hit the floor cold.

By the late 1940s, Handy and Chappo dead and buried, Charlottesville, along with the bits and pieces of what had gone on between them, behind them; both sisters were living up in New York with factory jobs and husbands. Velma was four months' pregnant with her third child and Maggie six weeks' pregnant with her first.

Velma had gritted her teeth when Maggie spouted the news and grabbed her hand to press against her belly. Maggie was beaming and Lloyd stood alongside her just as bright, not even a trace of guilt in his eyes.

How could he do it? She found herself still asking that question even as she forced a smile and agreed to plant some collard greens in the corner of her yard, because Maggie couldn't; she lived in a tenement in Brooklyn, her bedroom window looked down on pavement and garbage cans.

"Sure I'll do that for you, Maggie," Velma had said through clenched teeth.

"For the baby!"

"For the baby," Maggie agreed.

Now, Maggie, always clad in a housedress, black socks that climbed her calves and stopped at the knee, shaggy green slippers that hindered her already hobblelike walk. Head tied up and always smelling like liniment.

Fifteen years after the accident she was still mumbling to herself, hustling the children off to school in the mornings, passing out sneers instead of kisses after a night of weeping, and smoky dreams of the last time she laughed out loud and felt her husband's hands on her body, his breath against her neck. The mornings that followed those nights, and there were many, many nights like those, Maggie's mind would wander to the last day of smiles and laughter and an apricot sun shirking the horizon, Maggie in the driver's seat of that emerald green and white-topped Ford her husband Lloyd loved so, her belly swollen and low and barely able to fit behind the steering wheel.

She didn't want to drive, but Lloyd convinced her to go on ahead and do it because his head was bad from the Scotch Velma had put out special and just for him. Special and just for him.

Maggie didn't want to drive. Being in control of a machine that long and wide, unnerved her. She had trouble running the vacuum cleaner, for chrissakes.

"My head is bad, baby, go on and take the wheel. I'll guide you. It'll be fine." Lloyd was slurring and those eyes of his, those big brown eyes that had got Maggie all caught up with him to begin with, were bloodshot and half-shut.

"We could stay here with Velma. Go

home in the morning when you can drive."
Maggie spoke to her belly and pressed her
behind against the driver's side door.

Someone hollered out something from
the backyard and then there was a swell of
laughter before the music went up a notch.

Lloyd looked longingly over Maggie's
shoulder. The smell of marijuana and barbecue ribs wafted over the fence and Lloyd
inhaled deeply and smiled.

"You want to stay anyway, I can tell,"
Maggie said and pressed the palm of her
hand against his chest. God, she loved this
man, she thought to herself and moved her
hand to his shoulder and then down his
arm.

Their hands linked and Lloyd bent down
and gently kissed her cheek. The smell of
Scotch nauseated her and the baby kicked
violently inside her womb.

"You need to sleep in your own bed,"
Lloyd said and touched her stomach.
" 'Sides, I think I might want some to-
night." Lloyd gave her a sly look and
Maggie blushed and then giggled.

He still made her feel like a schoolgirl.

"You gonna drive, baby?" Lloyd reached
behind her and grabbed onto the door
handle.

"Yeah, okay."

She would remember how her hands looked, a warm bronze and clenched tight around the steering wheel, her wedding band choking her finger, hands swollen from pregnancy and the heat. B.B. King on the radio, the windows down and the wind pulling at her hair and making it hard for her to breathe. Lloyd leaned in close, one hand resting on her belly, the other thrown around the back of her seat, the feel of his warm breath against her face as he encouraged her on, persuading her to "Give it a little more gas. Just a little more," as they merged on to the highway and then the "Yeah, yeah, that's it. That's it baby, that's why I love you. That's why I love you."

Just hearing those words gave Maggie confidence and she pushed her back into the seat and pressed down harder on the gas pedal, moving into the left lane to take over a green Buick that had been creeping in front of her.

She would remember her laughter, hers and Lloyd's, entwined with the sound of the wind, the engine and B.B. King, the feel of the leather seat beneath her exposed thighs, the bobbing head of the brown-felt dog on the dashboard, but not the red brake lights of the truck in front of her or Lloyd's hand suddenly on top of hers, the abrupt jerk of the car as it lunged right, Lloyd screaming for her to brake, "Brake!" the shattering of glass and bending of metal as the car tore through the steel divider, the sick sailing feeling of flying through air without wings, and then the sudden impact.

Witnesses would report that the car rolled and bounced down the grassy knoll like a ball, finally coming to a stop, right side up. They didn't notice the smoke, not at first; they'd confused it with the billowing clouds of dust and dirt that mushroomed when the car finally came to its crashing halt.

They moved forward, slowly at first, their hearts beating hard in their chests and faces laced with shock. Then someone saw a spark of blue-and-white and then a yellow flame snaking its way from what was left of the front section of the car, along the sides and towards the back. Towards the gas tank.

Antoine Black and his brother Pedro were the first ones out of their car and down the slope, but turned back when they saw the flame. Walking backward a few paces before finally turning around and running, tripping over their feet and screaming for the other Good Samaritans and onlookers to get back. "It's going to blow!" Pedro screamed as he passed his brother, scrambling on all fours to scale the grassy incline.

Davis Browton, either, didn't hear the warning or just damn well didn't heed it, because he kept coming, even shoving Antoine out of the way when Antoine grabbed hold of his arm and tried to jerk him back. He kept coming because he didn't know any other way to live. Fifty-four years old, recently widowed, father of two and grandfather of one. His life had been one big uphill climb; he'd stumbled a number of times along the way, alcoholism, adultery, gambling, a yearlong bout with depression after his wife passed away from cancer. That had been the worse fall for him. Losing Cheryl had made him lose his grip on life and he swan-dived into a black oblivion.

But he'd eventually straightened himself out, with the help of his family, his sons, they'd helped him stitch it back together again, like a patch quilt, a piece from here and scrap from there. He was flawed but whole.

Davis kept coming because so many people had kept coming for him.

The smoke was thick by then, and the smell of gasoline strong, the flames licked out at him as he grabbed hold of the door handle, oblivious to the heat, his mind discounting the pain for the moment as he tugged and pulled and banged at the door.

He couldn't see in, had no idea if anyone inside was alive, but he kept at it.

Samuel Tyler joined in. Fresh out of the police academy, just married, baby on the way, his wife Amanda resting at home, a chicken baking in the oven, she wouldn't have let him go down that hill, she would have kicked and screamed for him not to do it, she'd loved him since high school, had saved herself for him while he sowed his oats through college and the year he spent working at his father's plumbing-supply business before finally tiring of that and taking the police exam and her hand in marriage.

She wouldn't have allowed it.

Together, Davis and Samuel somehow pried the door open.

They started on the woman first, pulling at her arms, squeezing their hands down between her legs, trying to dislodge her feet, yanking at the steering wheel, pulling and tugging until, miraculously, she came loose. Her feet were on fire; Samuel threw himself on top of them while Davis worked at trying to get the man out.

He was stuck good, but his eyes were open and he was screaming; Davis couldn't hear his voice, not above the sound of the flames, the sirens that were coming from every direction and the pounding of his heart in his ears. He couldn't hear his voice, but he saw the tears that swelled up in Lloyd's eyes and evaporated as soon as they spilled out and onto his cheeks. The heat was intense by then, the flames raging, Davis's arms were beginning to blister and he could see blood and bone where Lloyd's denims used to be, where Lloyd's skin used to be.

Samuel dragged the woman to the base of the incline. He yelled up for help, but the Black brothers were fear-stricken and that would not allow them to come back down again. Instead they backed away, pushing themselves further into the crowd and out of sight.

Two other men answered the call and they hustled down and carried Maggie as gently as they could up the incline.

Samuel rushed back to the car, his wife's face in his head, the scent of his mother's perfume suddenly in the air. "These are how last moments begin," he thought as he rushed forward.

The explosion propelled Davis, shot him like a rocket across the ground where he hit with a thud. The force of it sent Samuel stumbling backwards, but he did not fall, he just rocked on his heels for a moment and when the second explosion came, he fell to his knees and covered his eyes against the billowing fire cloud that blocked out the sun.

Davis, dazed, scooted backwards on his behind until someone in a uniform rushed over and threw a blanket over his flaming arms.

Velma Rose

Heroes.

That's what the front page of the *Daily News* called them. *Fatal* and *tragic* is how they described the accident. Maggie was dubbed, yet unidentified, as Jane Doe.

Front-page news and Velma's phone ringing off the hook the next day. Baby Audrey sick with the croup and Peggy and Bobby fighting over what to watch on television and now this.

"Girl, have you read the paper today?" Gladys screamed. Velma couldn't take any more screaming, Audrey had been screaming all night long. She started to answer but the doorbell was ringing, so Velma told Gladys she'd have to call her back and hung up.

She pinched Bobby's arm and popped Peggy upside the head as she passed through the living room towards the front door. They'd had each other in fierce headlocks, but she couldn't bother to separate them just then, the small assaults she'd dealt out would have to do for now. She covered her ears as she walked by Audrey's playpen.

Kayla Howard was standing on her front stoop, newspaper rolled up tight in one hand, while the other readied itself to press the bell again. Her face was tight and she did a nervous side step across the small brick step, reminding Velma of the caged cockatiels that sat in the window of the Rockaway Boulevard pet store.

Velma didn't much like Kayla Howard, her naturally curly hair and pinhole-sized waistline was enough to make any out-of-shape, married mother of three despise her.

"Yes?" Velma said after she flung the door open.

"You see this?" Kayla said and shoved the rolled-up newspaper at Velma. What Velma could see were Kayla's perky nipples poking through the thin T-shirt she wore, the gold chain around her perfect neck, and the beauty mark that sat in the center of her chest.

"That's Maggie," she said before Velma could take her eyes off of her and begin to unfurl the paper.

It was Maggie, bandaged and propped up in a hospital bed.

"Oh, my God" was all Velma could manage, before stumbling backwards into the wall.

"Where's Lloyd?" Those were Maggie's first words. It had been two weeks of touch and go. Every time the phone rang Velma expected to hear a doctor on the other end of the phone telling her that her sister was dead.

It had been the same with their mother, Chappo Hurston.

The waiting, while the cancer ate through her. The agonizing hours when she just lay writhing in pain and then the moments of madness when Chappo chuckled to herself and spoke to invisible visitors that fastened themselves to the whirling blades of the ceiling fan and sometimes the rounded steel foot rail of the bed.

Seventy-five pounds and still breathing on her own and every once in a while fighting off the nurses and her younger sister, Retha, who came to give her sponge baths.

"Tough ole gal," the doctors commented.

"I don't want to suffer no more. I wanna close my eyes and go home to the Lord, but y'all won't let me go!" Chappo screeched as she pounded her skeletal fist into her chest.

Velma wiped at her tears. She loved her mother and no, she didn't want her to go, but she didn't want her to suffer anymore either. "Mama, you go on ahead. I know you'll always be with me," Velma said and grasped hold of her mother's hand.

Chappo snatched her hand away and her eyes went cold. "I can't leave knowing things t'ain't right between you and your sister. I won't go 'til my family is a family again." She spat and turned her head away from Velma's hurt eyes.

"You two the cause of my suffering," Chappo whispered and pointed a thin finger. "You disowning your sista, telling people you t'ain't got no sista. What that say 'bout me? You and Maggie shared the same space in my belly, fed on the same tit. What you think that do to me when I hear you say them things?

"You 'low some man to come 'tween you, some man that made a choice with his heart. He just flesh and blood like the rest of us, if'n it wasn't done right, who you to judge? The Lord will take care of that."

Velma looked across the room and there standing in the doorway was Maggie and Lloyd.

"Them things in the past, how much time you got left? Anger eats up years faster than happiness, chile. You better get on with your living and forget 'bout that hurt. Hurt come and go, Maggie gonna be your sister

51

forever, no matter what you say. Family is precious, t'ain't nothing greater, 'cept God."

Chappo's eyes rolled in her head and she went quiet for a while as she fumbled with the sheet and struggled at clearing her clogged throat. She stared at the wall and then suddenly began to struggle to sit up. Maggie moved in, her hands stretched out to assist, but Velma had swooped down, and eased her hands beneath her mother's back, gently pushing her upright before placing a pillow behind her.

Maggie stood there for a moment, unsure what it was she was supposed to do with her hands. Lloyd knew, and enclosed them in his own.

Velma felt her head go hot and she had to beat back the anger that was bubbling up inside of her.

"Mama . . ." Maggie started, but Chappo swung a long scrawny arm at her. Maggie hopped back on her heels and Velma smiled smugly until she felt Chappo's hand weakly pushing at her chest. "Git back, ya too damn close!"

"My mama," Chappo began and then a coughing fit struck before she could go on, "My mama told me that you can't love your chirren' too close, too hard. All's it do is eat you alive when one of 'em does wrong or gets dead. I didn't believe her, but I knows now that is true."

"Where's Lloyd?" Maggie asked again when Velma didn't answer.

Velma snapped back to the present, her eyes wet with the memory. She dragged the tips of her index fingers beneath her eyes. "Uhm," she sounded when she could see Maggie clearly again. She still couldn't bring herself to say it, so she said nothing, pretending not to have heard the question, pretending not to know that Lloyd's body had been burned to cinders inside that car. Pretending not to have had their cousins Ollie and Aubrey haul all that brand-new baby furniture over to Goodwill and then her sitting down with Maggie's telephone-book and hers to call every single person that was supposed to come to the baby shower the following Saturday and tell them that there was no need, there was no baby coming and from what the doctors had told her, the damage to Maggie's womb had been so intense that they had had to remove it, every bit of it. However, there would be a funeral, Monday at ten.

Maggie wasn't aware of any of it. Her stomach was still swollen and she was high on morphine most of the time, so she just assumed (and because no one told her otherwise) that she was still pregnant and had even grabbed Velma's hand and pressed it against her stomach, "See, Velma, the baby is just fine, just fine. Kicking up a storm! Healthy and fine."

Velma had just nodded and smiled sadly. That baby was buried six feet deep in the earth. Velma herself had picked out the white coffin. The tombstone read simply:

Baby Girl George
1956

She'd started smoking again on the day of the funeral. She'd never buried anything so small, it had rattled her nerves and she picked the habit right back up, like she'd never even quit on Mother's Day five years earlier.

"Phantom kicks," the doctor advised Velma when she questioned him about it. "That'll happen for a month or so."

Two weeks later, Velma told Maggie that Lloyd was dead, Lloyd and the baby. She couldn't even look at her when she said it. She kind of mumbled into her chest, "Go on home to be with his maker," is what she said.

Maggie smelled the nicotine on her breath. "You smoking again, Velma?"

Velma's mouth went slack and she nodded her head yes. "Did you hear what I said, Maggie?" Velma leaned in and touched her sister's shoulder. "Lloyd is dead." Velma repeated herself. "And the baby too."

It pained Velma to say it. She had loved that man just as much as Maggie had. She had loved him first.

"It's bad for you, you know. Smoking. Cancer and emphysema. It's bad for you." Maggie fiddled at the blue-and-white crochet blanket Velma had brought from home for her.

Lloyd George should have been hers. She had never quite forgiven Maggie and certainly never forgot. She just buried the memory alongside her mother, and like Chappo's grave, she never forgot it was there.

Velma sighed and leaned back in her chair. "I know."

"Lloyd sure did love that car." Maggie spoke slowly. "Can it be fixed, Velma?"

Velma's chest heaved and straightened her back. "No, it can't be fixed, Maggie."

"He sure did love that car." Maggie repeated herself. "But he love me more!" she yelped and sat straight up in the bed. "He love me more, don't he, Velma?"

Velma dragged her hands down her face. She had children to worry about and a husband, trifling as he was, but hers just the same.

"Don't he, Velma?" Maggie's voice climbed.

"Of course he does." Velma sighed and patted her sister's hand.

"I ain't gonna mind if he loves the baby more than me." Maggie caressed her barren stomach. "I ain't gonna mind one bit, 'cause this baby got a lot of me and it's gonna be just the same, he still gonna be loving me."

Velma clutched her pocketbook in her lap and squirmed a bit in her chair. Her eldest son Bobby would be coming home from school right about now and her middle child Peggy would be running Chuck ragged, while baby Audrey Rose just slept.

She had laundry waiting and she'd forgotten to take the chicken out of the freezer. Chuck wouldn't think to do it, didn't think that he should. That was woman's work. Watching children was woman's work too, but because of the circumstances he would watch Audrey on his days off so Velma could go and visit her sister, but that would end as soon as Maggie was well enough to come home.

Maybe Bobby would take the chicken out of the freezer? Velma opened her bag and began to rummage through it. Her hands fell on her cigarettes, a tube of lipstick and then her small-change purse. She could call home and tell him to take it out and set it to defrost in a bowl of cold water.

Velma stood up and started towards the doorway.

"Are you going to call Lloyd? Tell him I'm missing him; tell him I'm sorry about the car."

Velma had just nodded her head.

"Maybe you can bring him a bottle of Scotch, that kind he likes, the one you set out for him that night, just for him. Remember, Velma?"

Velma stopped in her tracks. She was right at the door, had one foot resting on the beige-and-brown square tile of the corridor. She could hear the insistent buzzing sound of the fluorescent lights, the whispered conversations coming from the uniform-clad women at the nurses' station.

She turned slowly around. "What's that, Maggie?"

Maggie's face was free of reproach; her words hadn't even been malicious. She sat there staring back at her sister, blinking her one good eye and rubbing her stomach.

"He likes that Scotch, the one you always get special for him from Mr. Lucas. Double malt? I don't know." Maggie waved her hand. "You know the one, the same one you put out that night, the one he likes so much, the one you know he can't walk away from until every last drop is gone."

Velma narrowed her eyes and started towards Maggie.

She hadn't wrestled Lloyd's arm behind his back and forced him to drink the whole goddam bottle, she hadn't put a gun to his head. He was a grown-ass man, a man that claimed to know his limits.

If Maggie hadn't been so damn perfect, so blasted stupid, Lloyd would have been alive today, because he would have been married to her, and could have drank two bottles of Scotch if he wanted to and not have to go any further than their upstairs bedroom when he was done.

"What you saying, Maggie?" Velma's tone was drenched in venom as she inched forward.

Maggie just blinked, her face remained innocent, her tone childlike. "I said you get it for Lloyd, the Scotch, but you tell him it's from me." She looked around for her purse.

"That went down with the car too I suppose," she said moving her eyes back to Velma's face. "I got some money in the bank, I'll pay you back. Get it for him and say it's from me, you know 'cause I feel bad about the car. Get the kind he likes so much, the same kind you put out that night special for him."

Velma leaned in and looked dead into Maggie's good eye. "You trying to tell me something, Maggie?" Velma's voice dropped to a deadly pitch.

Maggie looked down at her stomach and then back into her sister's eyes. She cocked her head to one side and began slowly, "Yes, I am. I'm trying to tell you that I want you to get the Scotch for Lloyd for me. The kind he likes, the kind you —"

"Yes, yes, the kind I put out special for him!" Velma erupted in anger and threw her hands up into the air.

Maggie's head jerked back in surprise. "Yes," she whispered.

Velma walked three full circles on that brown-and-white tile floor.

She had her own children, frozen chicken, trifling husband, laundry — nearly two weeks' worth. Velma's mind whirled, she didn't need this; she certainly didn't need the blame, the guilt, especially not after

59

what they'd done to her. *Low-down, no good* . . .

"You should have just stayed over. You could have taken Bobby's bed. Lloyd could have slept on the couch. You didn't have to go. You could have just stayed!" Velma found herself explaining.

Maggie just blinked at her. She was dumbfounded.

Velma balled her fists and shook them at Maggie in frustration. "Lloyd is dead and it ain't my fault!"

Maggie pulled the crochet blanket up and across her breasts. "Get him the one he likes and tell him it's from me. Let him know I'm sorry, tell him to stop being mad and come and see 'bout me."

Velma squinted; there was pressure building behind her eyes, banging at the back of her head. She moved her palms to her temples and pressed.

"Maggie," she started again, but halted herself. What was the use?

Depleted, Velma leaned, shoulders slumped. "Okay, I'll tell him," she said.

Maggie smiled and allowed the crochet blanket to drop back down to her lap. "Make sure he come to see about me soon," Maggie yelled to Velma's swiftly retreating back. "Make sure now!" she added as

Velma disappeared down the corridor.

There wasn't anything left of Lloyd to bury, so his people came up from Charlottesville and wept over old photographs of him and fought with Velma about why it was only right that they should have the black-and-white console television, silverware, and a brand-new pressure cooker (still in the box) that Maggie had bought at Woolworth's a week before the accident.

Velma wouldn't allow it. The silverware had belonged to her mother, so it was only right that it remained in the family. Well, their family. Maggie and hers.

Besides, Velma had gone green with envy when Lloyd purchased that console for Maggie, she'd stopped speaking to Chuck for a good week, annoyed that he didn't run right down to Sears and buy her one too. No, no that console was hers and she wasn't letting it go. Dead son or no dead son.

Lloyd's relatives didn't visit Maggie at the hospital. Lloyd's mother, Ella, blamed Maggie for the death and incineration of her son and told Velma and everyone in earshot that she hoped Maggie would rot right where she lay.

Velma spoke up then, she had held her tongue all through the white rice smothered with ham hocks and black-eye peas, didn't even make eye contact when Ella reached for her fourth piece of cornbread and second helping of greens.

She'd held her tongue and when Ella grabbed up the pitcher of sweet tea and poured the last bit of it into her glass without even considering the empty glasses of the people who sat around her.

But now Velma had had enough of Ella's bad-mouthing and bad manners, and goddam it this was her house and her mama taught her to respect her elders but she also told her to protect her blood, and Maggie was blood, no matter what had went on between them when they were young girls.

By the time the red-velvet cake was put out and coffee offered Velma could hold her tongue not one minute longer.

Velma eased herself up from her chair and just stood staring at Ella and the rest of those no-account people she'd brought up from Charlottesville with her. She stared at the empty serving bowls and plates littered with bits of the food she had paid her hard-earned money for and then stayed up all night preparing and she thought about her sister laid up in Bellevue hospital, her feet burned and bandaged, one good eye, dead husband, dead baby, no womb, and leaned over to Ella and hissed: "Your son is the cause of his own demise. Lloyd never knew when to walk away from a Scotch bottle." Velma shook her head *no* and smiled. "No, I'm sorry. I'm wrong; he did know when to walk away, when it was empty. When it was bone dry."

Chuck covered his mouth and muffled a laugh.

Ella didn't even flinch. She was sucking cream-cheese frosting from her fingertips and looking around her to see who hadn't had the sense enough to hurry up and eat their slice of cake before Ella reached over and claimed it for her own.

"You right 'bout that Velma." Ella nodded her head in agreement and found the napkin she'd abandoned at the side of her plate sometime between the cornbread and the sopping up of the gravy.

She daintily dabbed at the corners of her mouth. "You right, he loved him some Scotch. Scotch and women must have been his weakness."

Chuck winced and his eyes slowly rolled from Ella's face to Velma's.

Velma's mouth opened and then closed and then opened again. Her palms were flat on the table and her fingers, which had been spread out like fans, were now clawing at the tablecloth.

"He liked to leave things *empty and bone-dry*." Ella yawned and ran the tip of her index finger down the center of the plate. "Wouldn't walk away from nothing or," Ella stopped for a second and considered her finger, speckled with cake crumbs ". . . anything till it was empty or in your case, used up and useless." Ella said and then dipped her finger into her mouth.

Not even a half a second fell between the last sounding syllable Ella mumbled and the moment Velma flew across the table towards Ella's throat.

Ella was old but agile, and the linoleum was clean and well-waxed, so her chair slid back effortlessly, allowing the flabby flesh of Ella's throat to skirt Velma's fingers.

Chuck moved just as quickly and caught Velma by her ankles with one hand, but not before the blue-and-white serving dishes, water glasses, crystal cake plate, and the last three slices of red-velvet layer cake, went crashing to the floor.

They left that night, Chuck holding Velma in the doorway as she flung cusswords at their backs while they loaded their suitcases into the trunk of the car.

The neighbors began to peek out of their windows and some even came out and stood

— hands folded across chests or planted on hip bones — on their porches to see what all the commotion was about. But that audience was short-lived because Velma turned her anger on them, just as they got comfortable, shifting weight from one foot to the other and looking around for that plastic garden chair they kept out front for just these occasions, and yelled, "What the fuck y'all looking at!" sending them scurrying back inside.

Where the bottle came from, no one knew, but it hit Ella upside her head and then hit the ground and shattered. Ella was more shocked than she was hurt, but howled out anyway, like her skull had been cracked wide open.

Her husband Edgar got real scared then, and so did the other three family members they had with them. Edgar's eyes bulged out of his head and then he mouthed something Velma was sure was vulgar before he gave them his middle finger and then turned around and bent over, presenting his scrawny ass to them.

Velma made a threatening lunge at them, even though she was fighting to keep her lips pressed together, but Lord did she want to laugh!

They hurried into the car, their eyes

trying to keep Velma in sight as well as check the sky for more flying bottles.

The car backfired once and Edgar screeched off before Ella could even get her car door closed. Velma laughed then, a raucous laugh accompanied by lots of thigh-slapping. Chuck just folded his hands across his chest and shook his bald head in dismay.

When the laughter finally simmered down to giggles, Velma wiped the tears from the corners of her eyes and asked, "Baby, who in the hell threw that bottle?"

No one saw Bobby creep across the roof and back through the open window.

Chuck shrugged his shoulders and looked up into the cloudless night sky.

When they brought Maggie home a month later, her feet still bandaged, her injured eye exposed, but swollen shut; Audrey was just starting to flip over in her crib and Bobby, just seven years old, had been picked up twice by truant officers and Peggy had taken to sassing Velma, no matter how many times she got popped in the mouth for doing so.

Chuck had cleared the den out. Wasn't much of anything in it, just an old dusty couch, forgotten keepsakes and boxes filled with old books and magazines.

Velma had tried to make it homey, make it comfortable and familiar. She moved Maggie's bed from the apartment into that room and the glass and cast-iron dressing table Lloyd had brought for Maggie when they got married.

"How you like it, Maggie?" Velma asked as Chuck wheeled Maggie into the room. "It don't look the same, huh?" Velma was beaming; she'd done good for her sister. "Chuck put some new paint on the walls and got the carpet deep-cleaned." Velma walked over to the windows and fingered the scallion curtains. "Remember these?" Maggie just stared at her. "Aunt Virginia sent these from Charleston two years ago. They were too long for the other windows in the house, but they fit perfect on these."

Maggie turned her head left and then right, using her good eye to take everything in. She understood now that her husband was dead, her baby gone. The realization blanketing her during the intervals when the morphine drip ran out and her body exploded in pain. Her head would clear and everything that had been said to her while she was floating on that ethereal high would be replayed and it was during those moments that she was able to comprehend that she had no husband, no child, an eye that might never see again and feet that were useful but scarred.

This was her reality now.

A year after the accident, Maggie got hold of a knife and slit her wrist. She leaked a quart of blood into the carpet. It's a smiling blotch of burgundy that Maggie won't allow Chuck to pull up, or Velma to disguise with a throw rug. Maggie says, "That's Lloyd's smile. Leave it."

So now the knives, butter, steak, and otherwise, are kept in a plastic bag, hidden in Velma's room.

By 1969, Velma's babies had had babies and the house was always brimming with noise, hardly ever a quiet moment to sit and read the paper or think about life. Some little one always begging for something, a cookie, a glass of juice, "Can I go outside please!" even on days when it was cold and the streets were icy, the patio covered in snow and the sky gray and sunless — there is no end to the pleading.

"No!" Velma would bellow and all the children would jump and scatter, even the ones who hadn't put in a request.

So many children and Velma's mind bothered with work and Maggie and money; so much so that most of the time she can't remember all of the children's names and so she just points and calls out to them by gender, "Girl, get away from that stove!" "Boy, don't let me have to whip you!"

There is no time for lovemaking, no privacy for it; Peggy's first son, Ivan, sleeps in between Velma and Chuck; his mother is living in Red Hook with her last two babies and new boyfriend Jovi, who won't raise a child that's not his.

All they want, all they pray for, is quiet and more than four hours sleep, but that's impossible, because Ivan wakes up calling for his mother every night and when he doesn't, Velma knows that he will wet the bed, so either way, their sleep will be interrupted.

Bobby has six children, ranging from ages two to eight, all from different women, and all claiming to love him and hate him. Bobby hasn't been seen for over a year, but women keep showing up at Velma's door presenting squirming infants wrapped in receiving blankets, button eyes, pug noses, tiny fingers pushing pulling and reaching out for her.

She knows they're Bobby's. She can tell, they all have his hairline, his tiny ears, and thin lips.

Bobby's two eldest, Jada and Hayden, stay with Velma full-time, their mother unable to handle them or too young to handle them with parents who contend that they've raised their children and ain't raising any more. The other three, Bobby Jr., Fleet, and Doris stay with her on and off, depending on the season, frame of mind, money, housing or just because.

Velma never says no, they are her grandchildren, her family, nothing greater, 'cept God.

She makes room, finds space, borrows money from her pension to remodel the basement into three bedrooms and full bath, goes without new clothes and shoes to make sure the children don't have to. Buys food in bulk and grows vegetables in the backyard.

She makes do.

Audrey Rose

"How's Audrey?" Family members call and ask, cousins that haven't been seen in years, uncles that last saw Audrey when she was still small and cute. Great-aunts that have school pictures of Audrey with lopsided ponytails and missing front teeth.

"She's fine. Just fine," Velma lies about her youngest child.

Audrey is nothing but trouble, with a capital *T*.

Seventeen years old, barely going to school, hating the place her home has become, children everywhere, like ants in her bedroom, in her bed. Toys littering the living room, under the dining room table, noise, so much noise. They get into her nail polish and 45's. Nothing is sacred to them. Nothing.

No peace at school either. The teachers always coming down on her, wanting something, giving something, keeping her after school, detaining her, she's got things to do. Things like Leroy Brown.

Leroy Brown. Tall, lanky, and black.

71

Hard-knot knees and sharp elbows. Leroy Brown all if nothing like his father, Wilfred.

That's why they hated each other so much.

Wilfred Brown, the in-and-out man. In and out of jail, in and out of a job, in and out of the apartments of single women who called his wife Tonya *"girlfriend"* and gossiped with her on the phone hours before Wilfred strolled into their apartments and propped his feet up on the sofa table like he owned shit.

Leroy Brown, just like his father, sweet on whatever walked, bounced, bent, and spread. Both of them favored the golden-colored ones, with the long hair and their "go on ahead," attitudes, the ones that never did slap hands away when fingers reached out to touch, stroke, unbutton, unhook, and remove.

Audrey Rose was one of those women. Honey-colored and poured into denim bell-bottoms that hugged her hips. Red-and-purple-patch butterflies riding the back pockets, pushing men to think about spring, newly turned earth, and sinking into soft pink insides.

Leroy had been Audrey's first, when she was still all nectar down in the between part of herself and she would only allow him to dip his finger in her hole and it came back wet and slick and sweet.

She could have had anyone of those tongue-lagging boys that followed behind her like dogs, but she wanted Leroy Brown; good for nothing and sneaky. A pickpocket and thief by age twelve. School just a memory by fifteen. Drinking, smoking, and in the streets, hanging with the wrong crowd, and arrested twice by the time he was eighteen.

Everything like his father, and some said, even a tad worse.

Two hustlers can't live under one roof.

They cuss each other first, the blows follow, Wilfred is the stronger of the two but Leroy has youth behind him and no matter how many times he's knocked down and slammed up against the walls, he keeps coming.

Although Tonya stands on the side, she is caught in the middle, trapped between being in love with her husband and loving her son.

There's a choice that needs to be made. Which love is fiercest?

Wilfred, lip cut and eye swollen, his years of bourbon and cigarettes beginning to show, beginning to wear him down, he's had enough, can't take much more, and pulls his straight razor from his back pocket.

Her heart should have leapt in her chest; she should have thrown herself between them. Some sort of motherly sacrifice should have been made, but she just stood there and God help her, all she could think about was the lie she would tell the police in order to keep Wilfred from staring out at her from behind twelve inches of glass on visiting day.

When it's all over and done, Leroy is holding together the sliced skin of his forearm while Tonya watches from behind the glow of her cigarette as he makes his way down the street, old blue pillowcase packed with clothes in one hand, high-topped black PRO-Keds knotted at the laces and roped around his neck.

Audrey walks the streets slick with leaves, stepping over pools of water, trying hard to keep her balance in her platform shoes. Tall and fine and oblivious to the soft rain that has started to fall as she pops Dentyne gum into her mouth and slides along. By the time she reaches the corner, gum wrappers are sailing to the ground behind her and her mouth is stuffed full with all five pieces of gum. She looks everything like a cow chewing its cud.

She's been with Leroy.

Leroy can't be left alone for too long, his eyes start to wander. That fast ass Simone Brooks wants a piece of him. Lisa Ferguson too. She can't risk being away from him too long, so she stops going to school and shacks up with him all day long. Giving him what he said he had to have or he'd come apart, "My dick will drop right off," he says and so Audrey lets him have her as many times as he needs to, and even when she's on her period. "Moses waded through a river of it," he says as he spreads the towel across the bed.

Now she walks along, insides aching, head spinning, every now and again lifting her hands to her nose and sniffing her fingertips and around the collar of her peasant blouse, but mostly she pauses beside parked cars to check her bloodshot eyes in the side-view mirrors.

Donning her shades, she pats at her mammoth Afro and makes her way down Rockaway Boulevard, towards home.

Velma still at work, Maggie is the first to greet her, not verbally, but with a nod of her head. She's got one of the little ones by his collar, pulling him back towards the dining room table and the unfinished homework he's left there. "You're late," Maggie says after she plops the boy back down into his chair and wags her index finger in his face.

Audrey says nothing. "You're late," Maggie says again and taps the top of her wrist. "Where you been?"

Audrey holds her head, her eyes are burning and she can still feel Leroy between her legs. All she wants to do is sleep. "At the library," she lies.

Maggie turns her head a bit so she can take all of Audrey in with her one good eye. "The teacher called here. You ain't been to school. Weeks now. Weeks."

Audrey smells the beef stew on the stove, the cornbread baking in the oven. She's hungry too, ravenous.

"That ain't true."

"You calling the teacher a liar?"

"Whatever," Audrey says lazily and moves past Maggie.

Maggie wriggles her nose. The children at the table go quiet and wait.

"You smell funny," Maggie says and shuffles behind Audrey, sniffing her like a dog. "You smell funny. Where you been? What you been doing?"

"Nothing," Audrey says and lifts the top off of the pot.

"Liar," Maggie says.

"Liar," the kids mimic and then laugh.

Audrey ignores all of them. "The cornbread ready?"

Maggie considers her. "White bread in the bread box. Cornbread for dinner." She moves in front of the stove and folds her arms across her chest. "Where you been, what you been doing?" She probes again.

"Call me when dinner is ready," Audrey says and moves past her again.

"No dessert for you!" Maggie screams at her back.

Audrey laughs. "I'm not one of the babies. I could give a shit about dessert."

"Ingrate," Maggie mumbles under her breath. "Fresh!" she screams at the top of her lungs after Audrey bangs her bedroom door shut.

The children giggle and Maggie sticks her tongue out at them before slamming out the back door.

Maggie's life is lived almost entirely inside of those walls. But she allows herself visits to the backyard; no one can mock her scarred feet or dead eye in that place where the grapevines race along the brick wall and the limbs of the raspberry tree spread out like wings, offering shade to the honeysuckle that has wrapped itself lovingly around its bark.

She'll take a few moments away from the children, away from Audrey's rudeness, and the smells of the stewing meat and imagine that she is beautiful again, whole and steady walking.

She closes her eyes and remembers.

"Maggie!"

Maggie's eyes fly open and Audrey is hovering over her, one of the little ones at her side, fingers gripping onto her denim jeans, eyes filled with water and bottom lip trembling.

Maggie looks at herself, legs pushed out straight like sticks. She tries to lift her head, but her neck is stiff, her mouth dry.

"Wake up!" Audrey yells and storms off, a crying little one scattering behind her.

They meet up again in the kitchen. There's smoke everywhere and a black pot in the sink, a pan of burnt cornbread beside it.

"You trying to burn down the house?" Audrey says and shoves away the little one.

Maggie turns her head and inspects the damage and then her good eye moves to the children, huddled together and scared in the living room.

She moves towards them, swooping up the frightened, crying one as she goes.

"You all okay?"

They nod their heads *yes*.

She touches each one. Presses her palm against their foreheads and cheeks. "We're all okay. We're all fine," she says and kisses the tiny one in her arms.

"Open the windows," she instructs Audrey and sits down to cradle the one she holds. "Stop shaking." She coos and begins to rock him.

For once, Audrey does as she is told.

It had happened, she supposed, in any number of places; up against the tree in the park, on the cot in his basement room, in the backseat of the Good Reverend's Cadillac. There hadn't been a rubber involved and his promise to "pull out" was never fulfilled, and so when a month passed and then two and no blood spotted her white cotton panties, she knew.

She told him between puffs of the joint they shared. She told him between sips of grape Concord and his pulling at her blouse, sliding his hands down between her legs.

"Really?" He coughed and then passed the joint to her waiting fingers.

"Yep."

"Ah, shit now!" he said and leaned his

head back up against the wall. He seemed to be happy; well, he was grinning. "That's wild," he said and ran his fingers through his hair. "A little Leroy Brown. Damn." He took the joint from her and inhaled deeply.

"Or a little Audrey Rose," Audrey said and she felt the giggles beginning to bubble in her throat.

Now she would have to tell Velma.

May slid in fiery behind the April rains, and blossoms every color of the rainbow speckled front yards. Dandelions poked out from between the cracked pavement of sidewalks and already the fireflies owned the night, so Chuck said there was no sense in waiting until Memorial Day to fire up the grill.

Velma was chopping up cabbage for slaw. The coals on the grill were glowing orange and Maggie was standing over it in a daze, staring down at the fiery embers, lost in a long-ago memory.

Velma's eyes swung from the cabbage to the window and every once in awhile she'd holler out to her sister, "Maggie don't get too close now, hear?" or "You all right? Why don't you come on in for a while? It's pretty hot out there." But Maggie never responded. She just stood there staring.

"Mama?"

"Uh-huh."

Velma didn't raise her eyes to meet Audrey's; she just kept chopping and fussing under her breath about Maggie. The children were tearing through the house, opening and closing the refrigerator, slamming the screen door.

"Mama?" Audrey ventured again, moving closer to her mother and resting her hip against the edge of the kitchen counter.

It felt strange, standing there next to her mother, Leroy's seed tucked deep into the bottom of her belly. She could claim the title *woman* now, childhood was months behind her. Chuck would have to stop calling her his little girl and Velma would have to show her some respect now.

Audrey straightened her back and cleared her throat.

"Yes, Audrey, yes?" Velma's tone was stiff. She stopped chopping to consider Audrey and then her eyes moved back to Maggie. "Why don't you take a step or two back, Mag?" she yelled.

Audrey moved a little bit closer. "I got something to tell you."

"Uh-huh." Velma was chopping again. "Is it about school, because I already know you're failing two classes. But I ain't gonna let that upset me on this beautiful day, so if that's what you gonna tell me, it's old news and we can talk about it tomorrow."

"Nah, it ain't that."

Velma stopped chopping, "Girl, do I send you to school to speak that way? *Ain't* ain't a word."

"Sorry, uhm —"

"Wait a minute, Audrey." Velma threw down the knife and leaned over the sink, sticking her head all the way out of the window. "Now Maggie, I ain't gonna tell you again. Get away from that grill or I'm gonna have Chuck put out that fire and there won't be any barbeque, now I'm serious!"

Maggie turned her head and blanketed Velma with a cold look. She took one step backward.

Velma sighed, "Thank you." She shook her head and retrieved the knife from the sink and began chopping again. "Okay, now what is it, baby?"

Audrey watched the blade cut through the cabbage layers. "I'm pregnant." The words shot out of her mouth in a rush of syllables. She took two steps back.

"Who's pregnant?" Velma absently asked. Her eyes were on Maggie again, who was taking itsy-bitsy baby steps back towards the grill. "I swear to God, she's worse than the goddam kids!" Velma bellowed and spun around and started out the back door.

Audrey drummed her fingers against the sink and waited.

"You wanna play with me?" Velma's voice climbed. "Fine, I'll play your stupid little game," she said and snatched up the pitcher of iced tea from the table and dumped its contents into the grill. "Are you happy now? No barbeque for you or anybody else!" she screamed and stormed away from Maggie.

The children groaned.

"Daddy, Mama had to douse the grill again!" Audrey yelled up to her father, who was just stepping out of the bathroom.

"Again?" he yelled back.

"Uh-huh."

"Goddamit!"

It's over the oven-baked barbecue ribs and chicken that Audrey mumbles out her situation again. Velma's attention, usually snagged on one of the little ones or Maggie, is free for a measly split second while her teeth worked at pulling meat from a bone.

"What?" Velma's face is comical. Her lips

smeared in barbecue sauce, bits of corn-bread caught in the corners of her mouth. Audrey almost laughs, but shoves a fork full of coleslaw in her mouth instead.

"What did you say, Audrey Rose Grafton?"

"Pregnant. She said she's pregnant," Maggie hollered from across the table.

Velma laid a hard look on Maggie. "I ain't deaf, Maggie."

"Well, you were acting like you are. Acting blind too, if you ask me."

Velma's jaw dropped. "What?"

"See there. Your ears clean, Velma?"

Chuck eyes bulged. "What you say, baby girl?"

"I said I'm pregnant."

Velma's mouth snapped shut again. "What?"

"Pregnant, Velma!" Maggie bellowed across the table.

Velma threw her hands up in frustration. "Shut up, Maggie!" she yelled and turned her attention back to Audrey.

"You ain't know, well, you must be blind, that child a good three . . ." Maggie stopped and looked hard at Audrey before continuing. ". . . four months gone by now."

Velma's eyes held fast to Audrey, who was staring down at her plate.

"That true, Audrey?"

Audrey just nodded her head.

"Well," Velma started and then she reached for a napkin and wiped at her brow. She had been through this before with Peggy. She didn't know why the news had sent her for such a spin. She was surprised it'd had taken Audrey this long to get knocked up.

"Who it belong to, that Brown boy?" Velma's voice was disinterested and tired. Another mouth to feed, another crying baby.

She reached for the bowl of potato salad. "Yeah."

It had been such a nice day, Velma thought to herself as she piled mountain after mountain of potato salad on her plate.

Chuck gently grabbed her hand. "Velma?"

"Leroy Brown," Velma mumbled to herself, "Ain't nothing but a low 'count no-good cheat."

Audrey said nothing.

"He can't hold a decent job. Lie through his teeth, rob and con. What the hell you wanna go and make a baby with something like that?"

Audrey opened her mouth to speak, but Chuck held his hand up.

"His own mama walk around telling the world he ain't shit. You know if your own flesh and blood got nothing but bad things to say 'bout ya, you must not be right."

The volcano inside Velma was beginning to boil and bubble, she felt the heat of the day on her neck, the weight of responsibility growing heavier on her shoulders.

Velma's nostrils flared. "You hearing me, Audrey?"

Audrey looked up at her mother and nodded her head.

"What you suppose to do about this . . . this . . ." She couldn't seem to find a word for what it was her daughter was carrying.

"Baby?" Maggie interjected.

"Shut up, Maggie. I ain't gonna say it again," Velma screamed and spittle flew across the plates of three of her grandchildren. The children exchanged glances and slowly pushed their plates away from them.

"Yeah, Audrey, what *you* gonna do about this baby, 'cause I'm already raising more than I can handle and you come in and add another?"

Velma erupted and slammed her fists down on the table.

"Don't worry 'bout me. I'll be fine," Audrey mumbled and grabbed at a napkin. "We gonna get married."

Chuck turned and looked at his daughter, his baby girl, his heart. God help him, he loved her more than the first two. He supposed it was because he knew all the while he was loving his wife, she was still in love with Lloyd George, moaning Lloyd's name in her sleep and sometimes when Chuck was up inside of her.

By the time Audrey was made, Chuck figured Velma was all his. That night he sank into her and she gripped his neck and called out "Sweet Jesus, Chuck," he knew then that his patience had paid off. After that night, she didn't look at Lloyd in that way anymore. That way that always reminded Chuck that he had been second choice.

Audrey came nine months later, but he knew even when she was still squirming up inside of Velma that that child was all his, Velma's thoughts had been only on him the night they made her.

"You gonna do what?" Chuck said.

"What!" Velma snatched the napkin from Audrey's hand and crumpled it into a ball. "You do and you'll regret it for the rest of your life," Velma spat.

"No I won't."

Velma glared at her. "Where you all going to stay?" Velma said and folded her arms across her chest.

Audrey had just assumed they'd stay there, well, just for a little while.

"Here," Audrey squeaked.

Velma flinched. She stepped away from the table and looked at her daughter from a number of different angles. "The hell you will!"

"This ain't just your house," Audrey said and looked at Chuck. "What you got to say, Daddy?"

Chuck was startled. No one ever asked him his opinion. There was no democracy under that roof. He was the man of the house, but hardly ever had a say.

Velma's eyes bore into him.

"Well, I —"

"Shut up, Chuck!" Velma screamed and started for Audrey.

Chuck jumped up from his chair and stepped between mother and daughter. "Now, now, Velma, ain't no need for none of that."

Velma looked through Chuck. "Move," she sneered, "I'm'a knock some sense into her sassing ass!"

"Sense, that's just what she needs," Maggie spouted.

"I won't," Chuck said and stood stock-still. "I don't see why they can't live here with us for a while. We lived with your mama before we got our own place."

Velma's head jerked.

Audrey stood and started backing her way towards the house.

"Velma just calm down, calm down," Chuck coaxed as he planted his hands on Velma's shoulders.

He could see it in her eyes, the rage. She wouldn't just calm down, Velma never just calmed down. She would have to break something, spit, or strike out in order to quell that rage, she would have to draw blood.

Chuck braced himself. "If you gotta hit someone, then hit me," Chuck said and braced himself.

And Velma did just that, socked him right in the mouth and Chuck hit the pavement with a loud thud. The children scrambled around him and there it was, a thin stream of red spilling from his mouth.

It was the engagement ring that did it. Who knew that a diamond chip could split a grown man's bottom lip in two?

"Pass the slaw," Maggie instructed one of the children and then she let out a loud guffaw.

Tonya Brown looked at her watch again. It was already close to two, and they had, from what she could see, ten to twelve more couples ahead of them. She had to be to work by four. She sucked her teeth in disgust and then dug deep into her brown-leather sack purse in search of another stick of Doublemint gum.

Velma watched her sideways. The short suede skirt, fake-fur poncho, and thigh-high boots. Who did she think she was, Pam Grier?

Velma chewed on the inside of her cheek and allowed her eyes to scale every inch of Leroy's mother and when she reached her face, their eyes met and Velma let go a smile that both she and Tonya knew was phony.

Tonya smirked back at her and threw in a slanted eye for good measure before glancing down at her watch. She didn't know why all this was necessary. Girls got knocked up every day and didn't get married. *"Shiiiit,"* she breathed and looked at her watch again. "What a waste of time," she muttered.

Velma's mouth was dry, she watched as Tonya popped a fourth stick of gum into her mouth. The fourth stick and she hadn't even offered her one, not one goddam stick!

Velma sighed in disgust.

In order to pass the time and forget about her dry mouth she counted the marble black-and-white squares of the city hall lobby and then the wrought-iron lanterns that hung from the forty-foot ceilings.

Nothing worked. All she could think about was her parched mouth and tiny house, packed tight with adults and babies. Audrey would remain there and Leroy would join her. It had been decided, but Velma couldn't remember just how. It had all happened so quickly and before she knew it Audrey was seven months pregnant and here they were down at city hall.

"Do you have any more of that gum left?" Velma finally holstered her pride and sauntered over to Tonya.

Tonya had looked at her strangely, as if Velma's question had been offensive.

"What?"

Oh, now she don't understand English?

"Gum, do you have another piece?" Velma felt heat pulsating around her ears.

"No," Tonya said and presented her back to her.

Velma considered snatching the horsehair ponytail off the back of Tonya's pea-sized head and decided it wouldn't be worth the aggravation and walked over to the water fountain instead.

"You nervous?" Audrey asked Leroy.

They sat on a bench just a few feet away from the pacing mother-in-laws to be. Audrey's left hand was resting on Leroy's knee while the other caressed her swollen belly.

"Nah," he said without looking at her.

"You don't want to do this no more, do you?"

He turned and faced her then. His eyes red from drinking all night and most of the morning. She could smell the Cold Duck coming through his pores. "Of course I do." His voice was tight and the smile he offered her, weak.

What was marriage? He supposed it was something you did when you knocked a girl up. It was something else you did when you got tired of stomping roaches and sleeping on a hard-ass cot in a musty church basement.

" 'Cause you don't have to, you know. Me and the baby going to be just fine without you." Audrey's lips curled and Leroy saw the Velma lurking underneath. He rubbed at his eyes and then jumped up and stuffed his hands into the pockets of his brown plaid pants. He hadn't even said "I do" and already she was nagging him. "Look here, Audrey," he hissed, "I'm here 'cause I want to be here. I ain't no jive turkey. I'm doing the right thing."

Audrey shifted uneasily and placed both hands in the small of her back. "Is the right thing what *you* want to do?"

Leroy looked at her and then began pacing the floor. "I already can't please you and I ain't even your husband yet!"

His words echoed through the hallowed halls and the security guard closest to the door gripped his billy club, shot him a menacing look, and took a step toward them.

"Y'all simmer down over there," Tonya called out as she unwrapped the last piece of Doublemint gum and shoved it into her mouth.

The house swells, bursting at the seams. Leroy is the weed amongst the blooms, the wildflower amidst the roses.

Velma says little of nothing to him, but her eyes scream volumes and all Maggie does is fuss, comment, and criticize under her breath. Chuck is trying, he engages him in sports talk, invites him to sit in on his card games, and explains to him what responsibility is.

Leroy pretends to listen, but his mind is on the street, the next hit on a joint, the swish-and-swirl sound of beer inside a bottle and then cold in his throat, the sweet thang with the wide hips and pretty eyes that said she didn't give shit whether he was married or not.

The children are another problem, they cling to him, jump on his back and holler, "Giddyup horsy!"

He ain't no goddam child!

There is the mention of money, contributing, holding down his end. He was never sure if they were talking to him, but those words always seemed to be in the air when he reached for the refrigerator door or poured a second bowl of cereal.

Leroy works sometimes. Petty jobs that seem to pay little to nothing but require incredible amounts of time.

Delivery boy for the butcher, unloading trucks at the Superette, cleaning the gum from beneath the chairs at the Rockaway Avenue movie house.

He can't keep any of the jobs for more than a few days. Meat goes missing from the butcher, can food and dairy products from the Superette, candy and a projector from the movie house.

By December, there was no work to be found anywhere. And he's tired of roaming the want ads and pounding the pavement in search of it. Work was a ghost and he was no conjure man, no spirit seeker.

Before he knows it, he's back on the

streets with his childhood friend, Earl Cannon, running scams and getting high.

So now Leroy has a plan that will put some money in his pocket. A plan that will keep the Roses' mouths shut for a while.

It's a good one. He and Earl come up with it in St. Clemmons Park, on the bench beneath the oak tree.

"You think it'll work, man?"

"Why wouldn't it?"

"I dunno."

"You don't know much of shit. I'm telling you, this plan is good. It's tight."

"Where you gonna get the truck?"

"We'll lift it."

"What?"

"Steal it, man. Hot-wire it."

"Yeah, from where?"

"I haven't figured that one out yet."

"What about the boxes?"

"That's easy, don't worry about that."

"What about the rocks?"

"Look around my brother, it ain't like they scarce."

"Yeah, yeah. You right."

"You think it's gonna work?"

"It'll work, trust me, it'll work."

Three days later, Leroy and Earl were on Jamaica Avenue hanging out of the back of a stolen meat truck.

"Hey, hey, my man!"

Leroy was the salesman; he had a golden tongue, honest eyes and a way with people.

"I got brand-new black-and-white televisions."

The man he'd stopped, an older gentleman with milky eyes and slow walk tried to ignore him and took a step around Leroy.

"Hey pops, wait a minute, hear me out." Leroy laid his hands on the man's shoulders. "You gonna pass up the deal of the century."

The old man swayed and looked around for a cop.

"I got thirteen-inch black-and-whites for twenty-five dollars."

The old man stopped swaying and looked deep into Leroy's honest eyes.

"You ain't gonna get that type of deal no place else. Believe me."

Leroy guided the old man towards the back of the truck. He rapped lightly on the door.

"Who is it!" Earl yelled from behind the door.

"Fool, its me," Leroy yelled back and smiled assuredly at the old man.

The steel door rolls up and there is Earl, surrounded by twenty-five large boxes.

"Another customer, huh?" Leroy grinned.

"Show him the product, Earl."

"Here we have a thirteen-inch black-and-white television. Zenith, hot off of the J.C.Penney loading dock," Earl said and slapped the top of the television that sat at his feet.

The old man's eyes go clear.

"Twenty-five dollars?" he asks.

"Yes, just for you my friend." Leroy laughed and clapped the old man on the back.

By the end of the day, three hundred dollars richer, bellies full and half drunk, Earl had to admit that, "Yeah, man, that was a good-ass plan."

The Good Reverend Panama knocked once and then pushed the door open. There they were stretched out on the basement floor of his church, half-grown men, looking like small children. Eyes heavy and faces scarlet with drink. Earl was staring upwards, but the Good Reverend knew that his eyes were seeing something other than the water pipes that snaked above his head.

Leroy also on his back, busy trying to stay awake, his eyelids fluttered when the Good

Reverend walked in, but the rest of his body remained still.

"My brothers," the Good Reverend exclaimed and reached for a forgotten wood chair. The wood creaked dangerously beneath his weight, so he hoisted himself forward, balancing himself on the edge of the seat.

He had been watching those two, knew all about their scams and petty offenses against the old, meek, and not-so-bright Queens residents. They were eager for money, pussy, and drugs. Those were the types of parishioners he wanted in his congregation.

Greedy, low-down, can't go a day without getting high motherfuckers that walked around like they knew everything, when the Good Reverend knew that they didn't know shit.

He had been like that once, but prison had taught him patience. The Bible had taught him faith.

He had faith in these young men and the mean streets that they wandered, he had faith in the harem of prostitutes that feared and loved him, he had faith in the Nigerians that supplied him with heroin, and he had faith in the power to be had and the money to be made from addiction.

★ ★ ★

"Boys!" he bellowed and clapped his hands loudly together.

They shot straight up and looked wildly around them until their eyes fell on the Good Reverend's fine, forest green, snakeskin shoes.

"I understand you boys pulled quite a scam today," the Good Reverend said and folded his hands in prayer. "I am proud of you, my sons," he said and then raised his praying hands up to the ceiling. "The Lord is proud of you because he understands why you did it."

Earl and Leroy exchanged glances, but said nothing.

"You," the Good Reverend pointed a long finger at Leroy, "you have a wife, are soon to be a father, and the Lord knows that the Man has kept you from securing a job. What else are you left to do?"

Leroy nodded his head in agreement.

"And you," the finger swung in Earl's direction, "why your grandmother raised you and now she's dying in some white man's nursing home."

Earl rubbed at his eyes.

"Bedsores, bad food." The reverend shook his head in disgust and Earl would swear on his dead mother's grave that he saw tears sparkling in that man's eyes. "You wanna see her some place better, some place where people care, right?"

Earl nodded his head and stuck his chest out a little bit further.

"My grandmama deserve better than that," Earl whispered and Leroy felt the crack in Earl's voice more than heard it.

"You damn straight she do!" the Good Reverend boomed and then clapped his hands together again. The sound split the air, and both Earl and Leroy felt their high slip away.

"Sometimes we may do wrong things." The Good Reverend leaned forward then, and the cuffs of his fine white pants climbed above his ankle and Earl saw that he wore no socks. "But the Lord knows we doing it for the right reasons."

"Hell, yeah!" Earl cried.

"Hallelujah," the Good Reverend said.

Maggie woke up suddenly and sat straight up in her bed. The yellow headlights from a passing car sliced through the thin curtains, slid across the wall, and blinded her for a moment before vanishing. Maggie blinked. She'd been dreaming about that night, dreaming about Lloyd and the baby that she was sure Velma had buried out in the collard-green patch. She wanted to go and visit with her now, but it was February and not one green thing could be seen sprouting out from the cold hard ground.

She sat there for a while, rolling the top of her blanket between her fingers and listening to the sounds of the house. The whistling noises of the radiators and the kick-start knocking clamor of the boiler. One of the children was talking in her sleep and Chuck was snoring in his.

She thought about the leftover pot roast and that evil little Ivan whispering to one of the others that she was retarded. She swung her legs over the side of the bed and clicked on the small bedside lamp. He was bad, that Ivan was, she thought as she slipped her feet into her slippers. She'd fix him, she mused, as she moved from the room, through the living room, dining room and into the kitchen.

Someone had left cracker crumbs on the table and a half-empty glass of — well, she wasn't sure what that was in the glass. She picked it up and sniffed. "Ugh," she groaned. "Beer." She dumped it into the sink. It must have been that Leroy. He was the only one in the house who drank beer in the middle of the week. The only one.

Maggie stood there for a moment, forgetting why she'd come into the kitchen to begin with. The wind howled and battered the side of the house. Someone's garbage can had got away, maybe theirs, helplessly caught up in the blustery gale. She listened as it rolled and thumped its way down the street.

"Ah yes, Ivan," she whispered, suddenly remembering what she'd come in the kitchen to do.

She went to the refrigerator and pulled off chunks of meat from the pot roast. Pulled from beneath it, so that no one would notice. She was almost done, content with the handful of scraps she'd acquired when someone started down the stairs.

She hurriedly closed the refrigerator door and looked wildly left and then right. What would she do? How was she going to explain a handful of meat?

"Maggie?"

Maggie stuffed the meat into the pocket of her robe and then opened the refrigerator again and snatched out the carton of milk.

"Maggie, what you doing?"

Maggie spun around. Audrey stood just a foot or so away from her. Her belly swollen and low, so low, Audrey had taken to walking with her legs wide open.

"Just getting some milk. Can't I have

some milk?" Maggie said and walked around her towards the cabinet to retrieve a glass.

"Sure you can," Audrey said and turned her body, belly first, to watch her. "But you don't drink milk," she said calmly and reached for the carton.

Maggie pulled the carton from her reach. "I do too."

Audrey sighed. "No you don't, Maggie. It gives you the runs." She took a step closer to Maggie. "Now let me have it."

"It don't give me the runs. That's apple juice."

"Apple juice and milk, Maggie. Both of them. Did you forget?"

Maggie hadn't forgotten.

Audrey shook her hand at Maggie. "C'mon now, it's too late in the night to be fussing."

"Then go on back to bed," Maggie said and moved backwards until her butt bumped the wall behind her.

Audrey's face contorted for a moment and then she pressed both hands on her stomach. "Look what you doing to me, Maggie, you getting me all upset and upsetting this baby." She spoke through clenched teeth.

"Good," Maggie spat and then turned the

container of milk up to her mouth and drank deeply.

They watched each other for a moment, Maggie's face wet and drenched in milk, Audrey gritting her teeth against the pain that was shooting through her body. "You, you just want attention," Audrey managed to say before she doubled over and inched her way towards the dining room chair.

Maggie followed her with her eyes and slowly set the milk down on the counter. "You sick. What? Baby coming?" She rushed to her side and began rubbing her back.

"You want attention too? What?" She pulled the chair out and helped Audrey into it.

"I don't want no damn attention," Audrey managed to say in between the deep breaths she'd begun to take.

"Let me go get your mama." Maggie started and Audrey grasped hold of her hand.

"No, no, don't leave me."

"Uh-huh, the baby is coming," Maggie said before easing herself down to her knees and pressing her head against Audrey's stomach. "I hear her in there, calling, calling," she whispered into the thin material of Audrey's nightgown. "I'm ready, she's saying. I'm coming!" Maggie whooped before planting a kiss on Audrey's belly. "We should go out back, out in the yard."

Maggie caught hold of Audrey's arm and started dragging her towards the back door.

"Get off!" Audrey screamed and knocked Maggie up against the wall. The pains were coming harder now, stretching across her back. "It's too early; I've got another two weeks."

Maggie rubbed at her hip and stared at Audrey.

"Get Leroy," Audrey yelled.

"What he going to do? His part is over now," she said.

"Leroy! Leroy!" Audrey screamed.

Leroy curled into a ball in the center of the bed, the tiny pinpricks that dotted his arm exposed beneath the streaming moonlight. It had been something of a curiosity to Audrey, she had ran her fingers over them and questioned him with her eyes, but he'd said they were mite bites he got from cleaning out the church basement and then reminded her how much he loved her before he sank into her, and she'd accepted that and soon after, forgot all about it.

No one had noticed the dazed look in his eyes or the roll and dip his head did when he sat in one place too long. Well, he was never around them long enough for them to notice. Out by midday and sometimes not back until long after midnight, Velma was just grateful for the few dollars he threw on the dining room table at the end of the week.

Now he lay there, shivering beneath the moonlight and hearing his name float around him, but unable to shift, except for his mouth, which was smiling because the Good Reverend had told him that he had to know and understand his product and that the nausea would only last a few days and then after that, it would be all good, all of the time.

And it was.

"He don't care. He don't care about the baby. What he going to do? What, what, tell me!" Maggie shouted. She backed away from Audrey, stuffing her hands down into the pockets of her robe. Her right hand closed over the meat and she remembered again that she had something she needed to do.

"You got plenty of time before she comes. Stop screaming, waking up the house. You just want attention," Maggie said and started off towards her room, snatching

Ivan's coat off of the coatrack as she went.

She was in labor for eighteen hours. Velma by her bedside, Leroy in and out, looking bored and staring at the white-stockinged legs of the nurses that came to check on Audrey.

"She's got a few more centimeters to go before she's ready," the doctor advised as he pulled the sheet back down over Audrey's legs. "Maybe by noon," he uttered as he snatched a quick look at his watch. "You really brought her in too early," he mumbled and walked out of the room.

Velma made a face at his back. She squeezed her daughter's hand and smiled weakly. "Don't worry Audrey; it'll all be over soon."

"Yeah, when?" Leroy said and jumped up from his chair. "I gotta be somewhere soon," he said.

Audrey moaned and turned to her left side.

"Ain't you got any consideration?" Velma hissed at him. "Your wife is about to give birth to *your* child."

Leroy sighed. "I can't do nothing for her now, can I?" He looked down at Audrey and Velma swore she saw disgust in his eyes. "I ain't being inconsiderate. I'm thinking about the money I ain't gonna make by sitting here." He dug into the breast pocket of his tattered denim jacket. The boy didn't even have a decent winter coat. "I need to make some money; I need to make some money to take care of my wife and baby. I ain't gonna make any sitting here."

He dug into the other pocket and then patted at the back pockets of his dungarees.

"You got a cig?"

Velma ignored his question. "You ain't got a job. Hustler is all you is."

Leroy shrugged his shoulders. "You got one or not?"

Velma turned her head and Leroy sauntered out of the room.

"Eight pounds, four ounces," Velma's tired voice said again.

"Sure nuff? Big ole thang, ain't she?" Chuck's voice was already heavy with pride and he hadn't even laid eyes on the baby yet. "Gonna play that number. Eight-oh-four."

"Hmmm," Velma sounded.

"What they gonna call her?"

In the phone booth, Velma lit a cigarette and exhaled. "You gotta call my work," she said and pulled deeply on the filter.

At home, Chuck rolled his eyes and looked into the mouth of the receiver. "Uh-huh. What they gonna call her?" He posed the question again.

"Some kind of flower name."

"Flower name, like what, Violet?"

"Nah." Velma rubbed her eyes and then blew her breath into the palm of her hand. Her head jerked on the rank return.

"Dammit," she muttered to herself as she began rummaging through her purse in search of a mint. Finding one, she popped it into her mouth and then sniffed at her armpit and caught the disapproving glance of a passing intern. "What the fuck you looking at?" she spat and threw her shoulders forward in mock attack.

"Velma?" Chuck pressed.

"Oh, Chuck, I can't remember what the hell they gonna call this crumb-snatcher!" Audrey's eighteen hours of labor had taken its toll on her patience.

Chuck remained silent as he listened to Velma puff on her cigarette.

"When you think you'll be coming home?" Chuck posed gently.

"Soon."

If it wasn't for the heart-shaped, red construction-paper cutouts clutched in elementary-school hands, flapping in the wind as the children made their way home, Valentine's Day would have passed Chuck by.

He took notice, though, and scrawled *214* beneath the *804* he'd written down earlier. He would play both numbers fifty-fifty every day until they hit.

That thought in mind, Chuck grabbed his jacket and bounded toward the door. If he hurried he could place it for the evening draw.

He swung the door open and came face-to-face with a brown face capped in blue. His heart sank. Bobby maybe or one of Peggy's boys.

"Yes, officer?"

"Are you Mr. Grafton?"

Chuck stepped cautiously out onto the porch and instinctively went to push his hands down into the pockets of his corduroys, but thought better about it and allowed them to fall obediently at his side.

"Yes."

"Ivan Grafton your grandson?"

Chuck felt his heart jump. "Y-yes."

It was then that Chuck saw Ivan's scared eyes looking out at him from the back of the police cruiser.

"What he do?" Chuck began to undo his belt buckle.

The officer's eyes dipped and then rose again. A wry smile caught hold of his lips and then he cleared his throat and brought one hand down on Chuck's right shoulder and began with:

"Nothing, sir, what happened was . . ."

Ivan was followed home by pack dogs that nipped at his legs and tumbled him over twice and then gnashed at the new coat he'd gotten for Christmas. The policeman had saved him by beating off the dogs with his club and then shoving Ivan into the back of the cruiser and bringing him straight home.

Chuck's eyebrows climbed his forehead in disbelief. "Really?"

He thanked the officer and ushered Ivan into the house. His coat was in shreds, the down filling spilling from open gashes left by the dogs' sharp teeth.

"What the hell happened?" Chuck asked as he helped Ivan remove his coat.

Ivan was dazed. He just kept shrugging his shoulders. He was trembling.

Maggie came out of her room. She had heard everything that had been said on the stoop. Her stomach was bad, turned upside down from the milk, but she managed a smile as she passed Ivan on her way to the bathroom.

From that day on, Ivan would believe that Maggie was a witch and he would never say another bad thing against her.

Camilla was a month old before Leroy showed up again; haggard-looking and thin.

"Where you been?" is what Audrey said to him after Chuck let him in the front door. She wanted to run to him, throw her hands around his neck, and then slap him across his face for leaving her. But Velma had talked bad about him every day since he'd disappeared and told her that she would be a fool to take him back. *If he came back,* so Audrey stayed put on the couch and worked the anxiety out through her fingers that clutched and unclutched the yellow-and-white receiving blanket she had begun to fold.

"I been in jail," he said and nodded across the room at Velma. Looking around the room his eyes couldn't help but fall on the bassinet in one corner, pink baby booties resting on the coffee table alongside the half-empty bottle of milk. The air smells like baby oil and Desitin and even Audrey's swollen breasts scream *baby* in the house, but Leroy acts as if he's still on cell block C.

"You got anything to eat?" He asks and starts towards the kitchen.

Audrey watches him, takes in the way his

112

jeans hang off his butt, the hair bumps black and chock-full along the back of his hairline. Her eyes find Velma's, who is chewing on her bottom lip and holding onto her anger best she can, allowing Audrey the space to be the woman she needs to be.

"Ain't you gonna ask about your baby?" Audrey spits.

"Oh yeah, where it at?" Leroy calls over his shoulder as he opens the refrigerator door and stares in at its contents.

"Wash you hands, boy, before you go into *my* fridge," Velma grinds out between clenched teeth.

"It's not an *it*. She's a girl," Audrey says. "She in the room with Maggie."

Leroy turns around suddenly. "With Maggie, is that safe?" he says, his eyes like saucers.

"Safer with her than she would be with you," Velma says and jumps up abruptly from the table. She gives Audrey one last look before heading up the stairs and into her bedroom.

Audrey waits for her to slam the door, but there's nothing, just the sound of the bedsprings wailing against Velma's weight.

Leroy finds a chicken leg wrapped in foil and the end piece of bread huddled in the vestiges of its plastic bag and decides that

that's good enough for now. His eyes search the side compartments of the refrigerator door, picking over half-empty mayonnaise and mustard jars (why don't they throw that shit out), a ketchup bottle, packages of soy sauce, and finally, the Red Devil.

"What happened to my beer?" he calls out to Audrey who's busy picking at her jagged thumbnail.

"You been gone a month, what you think happened to it?" she says before ripping the top of her thumbnail off with her teeth, and then as a secondary thought, "Don't you even want to know her name?"

"Whose?" he says as he settles himself down at the table and shakes some of the red-hot sauce onto the cold poultry.

One by one, the children begin to emerge from the place in the basement. It's close to noon on a Saturday morning and cartoons are all but over with. The sink is still piled high with bowls pooled with milk and speckled with Cheerios.

They stumble in, pajama-clad and hair a mess. The girls grip Barbie dolls while the boys hold onto miniature cars and medium-sized Tonka trucks.

"Hi, Leroy," they chime one by one as they pass him on their way into the kitchen in search of ice pops, cookies, and the hard

114

candy Velma keeps in a tin on top of the refrigerator.

"Hey."

Maggie emerges too, her eyes puffy from sleep. Camilla squirming in her arms, smacking her lips, and grappling with her tiny T-shirt.

"Naptime is over." Maggie yawns. "She's ready for that tit," she says and bends down to hand Camilla over to Audrey and when she straightens up again, her head snaps around to Leroy. Her mouth opens and then closes and then her eyes narrow.

Leroy is folding a blanket of bread around the chicken leg. He looks up and their eyes meet. "How you doing, Maggie?" He greets her and then throws her the peace sign.

Maggie folds in her bottom lip and cocks her head, she takes, one, two, three paces and then bends forward a bit. She sniffs the air and then lets go of Leroy's eyes to look down at the chicken leg and bread.

"You come in here with that?"

Leroy's lips part a bit, but not a sound comes out. He shakes his head *no*.

"You get that from the fridge?"

He nods his head *yes*.

"That's mine, then. Put it back," she says and straightens her back.

"But I —"

"Put it back," she says again and her hands ball into fists.

"You better do it," Ivan whispers from behind him, "or she'll sick devil dogs on ya."

The Good Reverend Panama stood at his altar staring out at the rows of empty folding chairs. He grinned. Soon, his parishioners, his followers, would file in and fill those chairs, digging deep into their pockets; they would also fill the baskets with their hard-earned money. His grin stretched into a wide smile.

He'd worked up quite a sweat, hollering and screaming, yelling the word out and thumping his Bible. He'd even been able to squeeze out a tear or two before speaking in tongues and then collapsing over the altar. That little piece of theater had brought the congregation to their feet.

Two women in the middle row fainted straight away and Harper Singleton, an old drunk who'd lost his wife and mother both in the same year, fell down on his knees and started wailing: Lord, Lord, Lord!

The Good Reverend Panama liked that type of enthusiasm.

Leroy appeared on cue from behind a

wall beyond the altar and threw a sweeping, blood-red velvet cape over the Good Reverend Panama's limp shoulders. He dabbed his forehead with a matching velvet handkerchief and carefully, gently shook the Reverend until he was conscious enough to be guided to and placed on his throne.

The church fell quiet. The parishioners leaned forward and held their breath.

Leroy walked to the edge of the stage.

"God has spoken to the Good Reverend Panama and his message is," Leroy took a moment to clear his throat and pop the crick in his neck before he continued, "silver never did nothing positive for nobody 'cept fill a cavity."

The parishioners' faces went blank and they began to mumble and shrug their shoulders in confusion.

After a while, Leroy cleared his throat again and held his hands up to silence the crowd. "God don't wanna see no change in the baskets this Sunday."

The crowd groaned.

Leroy looked unsure and turned his gaze to the Good Reverend, who remained lifeless.

Leroy turned back to the crowd. "When you give the Lord give back," and Leroy thrust three fingers out at the crowd, "three-fold!"

A low grumble rolled through the congregation and slowly, almost painfully the metal lips of pocketbooks were unclasped, billfolds were pulled from back pockets and greenbacks, rolled cigarette-thin, magically appeared from the dark narrows of cleavages.

It came to him as he watched Camilla sucking happily on Audrey's nipple. It occurred to him because this house wasn't such a bad place to be, when he had to be there. Soft bed, hot water, and Audrey to roll over on whenever he wanted, well lately, whenever he insisted.

It knocked into him like one of the little one's balls, thumping up against the toe of his shoe as he sat on the couch and tried not to nod as he held Camilla while Audrey was off tending to the laundry or something on the stove.

The thought thumped against his brain, snapping him straight for a moment long enough to realize that Audrey didn't look at him the way she did just a year ago when all he was doing was begging and she wouldn't let any part of him but his finger up inside of her.

And now she had little to nothing to say to

him and when she did talk, it was all about the baby. *The baby this and the baby that.*

"What about me?" he'd asked myriad times.

All he got were looks of contempt, a flat back, and the saucy swing of her behind as she stormed away from him.

What had happened to that golden-honeyed thang that could down a forty in fifty, roll a joint tighter than he ever could, and who had lifted her skirt, bared her ass in broad daylight (the invitation implied) when the Garcia sisters from Lefferts Boulevard called her a "stuck-up bitch!"

What had happened to that girl?

Motherhood had happened.

Audrey moved with the other women of the house now; those women that despised him for just being born.

Leroy watched them, huddled together at the stove, over the sink, whispering about who knew what and then the laughter as buoyant as the bath bubbles Camilla splashed happily about in.

Giving birth had bestowed Audrey with thorns and had brought her closer to mother and aunt.

It occurred to him that he had to get her back before he could be plucked and cast out of Eden.

★ ★ ★

She didn't like needles. "Uh-huh," she said as she laid Camilla down into her bassinet. She hadn't pulled her T-shirt down or pushed her breast back into her bra, and he watched, almost hungrily as a tiny droplet of milk dangled from her nipple.

"Audrey, you ain't never had nothing like it. Believe me," he said, stepping closer to her, but careful not to touch her.

"Nah, you know I don't like needles," she said and finally put her breast away and pulled her T-shirt down.

"C'mon, just once, just for me?"

Audrey moved onto the bed and scooted backwards until her back was against the wall. The pink-and-white bedspread shifted, revealing the white sheet beneath.

"You lied to me, Leroy."

"What?" he said and pushed his hands out before him. "What'd I lie about?"

"Those marks on your arms," she said, pointing at his arms.

"I didn't lie," he said and waved his hand at her. "That was the truth. I just started doing this shit last week."

Leroy moved onto the bed. "You actin' like you too good to get high with me."

Audrey just shook her head.

"Damn, we usta get high all of the time

and now you actin' like I'm a junkie or something."

Audrey turned and looked Leroy full in the face. His eyes were yellow and his skin had taken on a gooselike tone.

"I ain't say you were no junkie." Audrey breathed and then looked down at her hands. "You know I don't like needles, Leroy."

"I'm a make sure you don't feel a thing, baby. Trust me."

Audrey didn't allow him to needle her. She just couldn't stand the thought of it and he didn't mention it again for a few days. But then, in the smoky back row of the Rockaway Boulevard movie house, three of the little ones two rows ahead, squirming about in their seats as Bruce Lee kicked and tumbled his way through a mass of black-clothed bad guys; Leroy pulled out a sack of it and dangled it in her face.

"You can snort it if you want," he whispered as he ran his hand up her thigh. "It's better that way anyway," he murmured as his fingers began to fumble with the zipper of her jeans.

She turned and looked at him, her husband, this boy-man that claimed to love her. "Will it hurt?" she asked.

"Nah. You gonna feel on top of the world." He sniffed and rubbed at his nose. "C'mon," he pushed.

She watched as Leroy untwined the small plastic bag and dumped a bit of the powder into his palm. "Just a little bit, okay?"

On the screen Bruce Lee kicked a man through a plate-glass window and the theater roared with approval. The little ones climbed up into the seats and began jumping about, kicking at the hazy darkness.

"Sit your asses down!" Leroy screamed at them and across the aisle, a group of teenagers laughed out loud.

Audrey bowed her head and sniffed.

Seven seconds and Audrey is floating above the red-velvet seats, she sees a man in a dark corner, his hands stuffed down the front of his pants, his head thrown back, eyes closed, his face twisted in pleasure. There's a couple close by, oblivious to what's happening on the screen, they kiss feverishly as their hands slowly caress damp places beneath the other's clothing.

Audrey floats right into the movie and then far beyond that into a field, where the air is warm and her feet are bare, and she is dressed in a sarong the color of leaves and although she has never been to that place before she knows that it is Mesopotamia and that she is suddenly Sumerian and the sweeping field she has wandered into is *Hul Gil*, the joy plant.

In that place there are no homes that grow people, no pink-skinned newborns and pissy diapers. No want or worry at all, just bliss and warmth. Audrey wants to stay in that place forever, and so half an hour later during feature film number two, she dips her head again.

Things begin to disappear. The good china and heirloom silverware, Velma's wedding ring, the one she hadn't been able to fit since she'd given birth to Peggy, the one she had wrapped in toilet paper and placed beneath the bag of knives in her bottom dresser drawer.

All of those things walk right out the door like the teacup and saucer from that Disney movie Velma had taken the kids to see. It was all the children could talk about when they came back home, T-shirts blotched and spoiled with popcorn butter.

Bobby's daughter, Doris, as small as she was, had gotten into the utensil drawer and lined up all of the forks and spoons on the floor and sat down and waited for them to get up and walk away. She'd begged for the teacups and saucers, but Velma shooed her away and told her to stop her nonsense.

Doris would have begged for the teapot if they had one, but currently, they boiled their water in the same pot they cooked the rice in.

They didn't notice they were being robbed blind until Chuck opened his wallet to hand a dollar off to one of the little ones and he realized that all the twenties and tens were gone. And then Velma eyed the change jar that sat in the corner of the dining room and saw that only pennies remained, and very little of those.

The children are questioned first, even though Chuck and Velma know the truth. They take the little ones and interrogate them separately. They threaten and cuss, keeping the coiled leather belt in view.

The children stammer and some cry and admit to snatching up forgotten candy left on the sofa table, and even a dollar here and there, and yes, yes, they've dipped quarters from the money jar, but never enough to notice and never ever silverware.

Ivan just shrugs his shoulders, what's the sense in even speaking; he thinks to himself, he gets blamed for everything, anyway.

Some get pinched, others, thumped upside the head and one or two a quick lick on their backsides, the sound of the belt against their bottoms, more unpleasant than the pain itself.

When they caught Audrey in Mays Department store, she had four bras hooked over her own, socks stuffed in her coat pocket and two blouses rolled and tucked into the waistband of her jeans.

She was almost out the door, but was delayed doing a side-to-side shuffle with the old woman who was trying to come in. The security guard had grabbed her by the elbow just as she stepped around the old woman and caught sight of Leroy hunched over against the March wind, trying to light his cigarette.

He saw her too, but then looked the other way when he saw the security guard.

Leroy wouldn't see her again for another year, and when he did, she would be dancing; flinging her arms about her head, gyrating and twisting her pelvis, lost in the music and oblivious to the men at her feet, the ones slapping their hands against the shiny floor of the stage, yelling her name and beckoning her with dollar bills and wagging tongues.

Velma wouldn't go down to the hearing. She had been to all three by the time Audrey was picked up the fourth time. She couldn't stand to see her own pained expression looking back at her as she applied her mascara and lipstick, readying herself to go to court. She told Chuck that she would not go, not again, and so he would have to, if he wanted to. "I really don't care no more."

"You don't mean that, Velma," Chuck had said.

She already knew from the last time Audrey was caught shoplifting that if she was picked up again, she would do a minimum of six months in Riker's. So really what was the point of going, they already knew the outcome.

Chuck went and came back angry, like the sentencing was a surprise. He punched a hole in the wall and then went out back to drink away the pain.

Camilla was two years old by then.

It was there, in the female section of Riker's Island, twenty women, one toilet, thin sheets and scratchy blankets, that Audrey first shot up, and first made love to a woman.

Audrey had done thirty-day stints at

Riker's three times in the last year and a half, but her court-appointed lawyer had avoided her eyes and shook his head *no* when the judge asked him if he had a defense. A bang of the gavel and Audrey turned and saw the heartbreak in her father's eyes. *I love you* would have been appropriate, but Audrey mouthed: "Don't come and see me," instead.

Thirty days had been easy to do. The drugs were always plentiful; as long as you were willing to drop to your knees and do what the male guards wanted you to do. Audrey hadn't had a problem with that. She would just imagine herself elsewhere, blocking out the painful hardness of the cement floor beneath her knees, the masculine, manipulating palm pressed at the back of her head, the scent of them, the taste.

Six months seemed easy until day ninety rolled in. By then her knees were raw, her jaw tight and the back of her throat covered in white blotches that made it hard for her to swallow.

Selena Olivier. Nutmeg in color, with long, wavy, black hair.

Barely five feet and stout, it was her tiny waistline that saved her from being called fat. She walked on her toes (a habit she'd never broke from childhood) and could care less about what people said about the excessive body hair (they called her jungle legs and Grouchette Marx), and she used the word *cunt* as casually as most people exercised, *hello*.

Selena had people everywhere in that prison. Uncles that worked for correction, cousins on neighboring cell blocks, in neighboring cells and that alone is what kept her from getting knifed in the shower, jacked-up behind the bookshelf in the library and getting her way.

She wanted her way with Audrey and let that fact be known to the butch girls that wore coiled bandannas around their foreheads, pumped iron, and tucked cigarettes behind one ear.

Selena courted Audrey as hard as any woman could behind bars.

Her gifts were measly at first. A fruit cup from dinner, an extra biscuit at breakfast, all presented with a smile and small talk.

A bottle of perfume left under her pillow, a brush for her hair, extra socks.

The gifts gain her time; the conversation exposes Audrey's weaknesses, allowing Selena to get close to where Audrey's joy lived.

In the yard, Selena presses a bag of heroin into Audrey's hand, and then bends to kiss her cheek. Selena smells the perfume on her neck, knows that Audrey has groomed her hair with the brush. Audrey crosses her legs and smiles, the top of the white socks gleam out from beneath the cuff of her jeans.

Selena is making headway, she is confident the next kiss will be on the lips.

Audrey supposed it could have been a romantic and touching thing, if it wasn't for the other eighteen pairs of eyes watching them and the thin narrow mattress that could hardly accommodate one adult body, not to mention two.

Could a kiss be that soft, that tender? Selena's mouth told her it could be and Audrey rolled onto her back and allowed Selena on top of her, their mouths locked together, tongues dancing, their bodies rubbing, rubbing until Audrey exploded and then still, Selena would not stop giving and eased down so that she could kiss Audrey between her legs too.

They are released just days apart. Selena first and Audrey later that week on a Thursday. Selena has a place uptown, east Harlem, *el barrio*. Audrey has a love for

Selena, no fear of needles now.

It was her brother's place, but he was never there; well, hardly ever. "You will come and stay with me for as long as you want," Selena said, her hands lovingly cradling Audrey's face. "We could make love all day long, *chula,* if that is your wish," Selena curls out on her Dominican tongue.

Yes, yes that was one of Audrey's wishes.

The two eat beans, yellow rice, plantains, and baked chicken. Spend hours at the local hole-in-the-wall, throwing back rum and cokes and flirting with beautiful, dark-haired, smoky-eyed men with hips that swivel.

Audrey doesn't even think twice about them, the men. Selena is all she thinks about, Selena and the needle they will share later on and the love they will make after that.

By the time winter comes nuzzling in, there are other women coming and going, men too. They sleep with Selena and sometimes reach for Audrey when her head is rolling on her neck, the needle stuck in her arm. Audrey smiles back and allows them to remove the needle, kiss her lips, touch her beneath her shirt. They utter, *"ay, mami"* as they handle her like a rag doll, manipulating her arms to hold them.

The men are less affectionate; they take her wherever they find her and most times they don't even take off their pants, or know her name. Sometimes they leave money, but Audrey's not even sure of that, because Selena snatches it up just as soon as it is laid down.

Audrey is only concerned about the drugs and the love she has for Selena. But during the clear moments, the space in time before the next hit, Audrey wonders if Selena still loves her, because lately it seems as though her love is as invisible as the air they breathe.

"Do you still love me, Selena?" Audrey asks as she reaches for the belt to tie off her arm. There's no response but Audrey takes Selena's heroin nod for a yes.

She hadn't forgotten about her, even though Chuck was sure she had. "How could I?" she said whenever she saw that look on his face.

Six months and no word at all from Audrey.

"You only remember when you pass the barbershop and see the missing-persons flyer sitting in the window," he accused.

Chuck had gone to meet Audrey on her release date. She had sent a letter telling

131

him when and at what time. He'd paid a neighbor ten dollars to borrow his black Pontiac so he could pick his baby girl up and bring her home in style. Like a ride home in a borrowed car could magically make the last six months disappear. Like leather seats and cruise control could erase disgrace. Velma just *humphed* but didn't say a word until after Chuck splashed on the Old Spice and asked her again if she might want to come along. "I ain't taking a day off of work to ride up with you to get *her*. Now don't ask me again."

But the correction officer had just blinked his gray-green eyes at Chuck before checking his release sheet for the fourth time. "No. I don't have an Audrey Brown being released today."

Chuck felt his stomach flip and thought that his breakfast of pancakes and bacon would spew out all over the young man with the green-gray eyes. Chuck scratched at his chin. "Well, could you check when she will be released?"

All a waste. "Ten dollars and two and a half hours' drive, each way, plus gas and tolls? Fool, I told you so." Velma's voice had already started to punish him in his head.

Maybe he had read the date wrong,

maybe Audrey had written it down wrong in the letter.

The officer came back from a bank of steel filing cabinets located in the corner of the room; he had a sheet of paper in his hand. "Oh, here's the problem. Audrey Rose Brown was released a week and half ago."

It was funny, Chuck thought to himself as the officer's hands flew up, blocking the full horror that hung on his face, *pancakes and bacon tasted the same way coming up as they did going down.*

"That's not true." Velma continued to defend herself. "There's the flyer in the beauty-shop window and one on the telephone pole on a hundred-and-twentieth. I remember when I pass those flyers. I remember then too."

Velma had meant it to be a joke, even though it was a bad one. Maggie had laughed, but Chuck had just turned and walked away.

"He got Peggy. What he so mad about. He still got one daughter left," Maggie squawked and then got up and started behind Chuck. Mocking his lumbering walk and the way his body had started to lean forward as he got older.

Chuck had turned on her, fists balled, eyes narrow and menacing. "Not today, Maggie," he'd managed to say without anyone seeing his teeth.

Maggie had laughed, but not taken that step backwards that Chuck needed her to take and Velma thought for one horrible moment that he would actually hit her.

"What?" Maggie asked, her tone challenging him, daring him to do what his eyes told her he wanted to do.

"Stop it," Velma demanded, trying to keep the nervousness out of her voice. "Sit down, Maggie, and stop acting stupid."

Maggie didn't move and Chuck finally turned and walked away.

"Leave him alone, Maggie, stop riling him up."

"You the one that don't remember, that's what making him mad, not me," Maggie had huffed and walked off to her room.

How could either of them believe that she had forgotten about her child? She'd carried Audrey around inside of her longer than any of her children. She was two weeks' past due when the doctor finally told her to drink the castor oil that finally brought on the contractions.

Besides, Audrey was her baby. The last

one before the doctor pulled out her insides and told her that would be it for children, but she was lucky, he said, "God had blessed her with three."

She hadn't forgotten about her. She dreamed about her almost every night, prayed for her between breaths and saw her eyes in the faces of strangers she rode the train with.

What was she supposed to do? Walk around weeping and fretting every day? She had two other children to worry about; she had grandchildren depending on her. She knew how to keep her pain hidden; she knew how to love her children at arms length so that something like this didn't unravel her completely. She knew that she wasn't supposed to love her kids too close or too hard. Chuck had better learn to do the same.

No, she hadn't forgotten about Audrey, how could she with Camilla walking and talking now, keeping up as much as she could with the other ones, calling her "Vella" and Chuck "Pop-pop" and looking everything like Audrey.

How could she forget her?

The sun was low and brutal on that July 12 day. The heat bullied everyone back in and behind the steel doors of the brick-faced homes whose white owners had suddenly found themselves neighbors to brown-skinned families who had paid too much for the board-and-shingle houses with walls that rattled in high winds and roofs that cried in storms.

Those people, the brown ones, talked loud and found any reason to barbecue and play the blues, they set their speakers in the front windows while they lounged on old car seats that had been ripped from the backs of Oldsmobiles and Cadillacs that would spend their last days propped up on cinder blocks in driveways rusting away beneath the promises of repair.

Oblivious to the FOR SALE signs that sprout in their white neighbors' front yards amidst the delphiniums; they dig deep, the brown people, into pension plans or take out high-interest home-equity loans in order to put up aluminum siding so they could walk with their heads just as high as their white neighbors, while pretending that they understood the reasoning behind a gravel driveway when all they really comprehended (and desired) were the above-ground pools.

On that day of unrelenting heat when yet

another moving van carted away the twenty-year-old insides of a sixty-year-old house that had seen a family of Gianaris as well as a family of Ferraros and would now house a family of Lincolns — there were four fans running in the living room alone. Velma on the couch, a piece of old sheet wrapped around her to keep her cool, but that was already soaked through with sweat as she worked on corn-braiding the hair of the child that sat patiently between her legs.

That little one doesn't, even notice the heat and it seems as though neither do the ones whooping it up out in the backyard.

Maggie shuffles through and, even in the heat, her feet and calves right up to the knee are clad in wool socks.

Velma shakes her head and dips her finger in the Dixie Peach grease, swathing the scalp bared by the part she's just made in the small one's head before starting another cornrow.

When the phone starts ringing it just adds to the heat and her irritation. Velma's halfway done with the braiding and the sweat is pouring down her face and dangling from her chin. She's cursing the plastic on the couch and Maggie is just standing there, staring out into the yard, yelling at the children to keep away from her collard greens.

"Answer the goddam phone, Maggie, please!" Velma screams and snaps the comb on the curious fingers of the little one between her legs.

Maggie says hello, but not much else. She nods her head for the rest of the conversation and places the receiver back in the cradle before walking into the living room and blocking the whirling blade of one of the fans.

"Who was it?" Velma asks without looking up from the head of hair she's working on.

"Someone called," Maggie says.

"Yes, I know. Who was it?"

"Ask for you and then Chuck."

"Maggie, who the hell was it?"

"Said, Audrey is . . ."

The sound of her daughter's name is like sirens and Velma's fingers slow to a crawl and then stop. Her heartbeat quickens and fades, quickens and fades and then there is a moment of wonder as she realizes that anguish and fear have a taste, because it's backed up and sour in her throat.

Velma thinks about her mother and father and the orange blooms from the rosebush she sprinkled down into their graves and is reminded of the weeping that went on over Lloyd, even though there was no body.

She thinks that she hasn't had to bury anybody in years, but the thought springs the emotions that come along with death and it's just yesterday that an aunt died, an hour ago that she lost her mother. The years burn away and it seems as though just seconds have passed since Velma laid a carnation across the top of the tiniest coffin she had ever seen.

She sucks in air and the comb drops from her already shaking hands, as her heart clamors inside her chest. Everything she is fights against hearing what it is Maggie has to say, but Velma finds her body leaning forward anyway even though her mind is screaming, "Wait, wait, I'm not ready yet!"

She nods her head at Maggie, a gesture that says, "Go ahead, give it to me straight," and waits for the words that will tell Velma that even though she thought she was doing the right thing and the best things she could, she had been all wrong and this was her punishment. The comb drops from her hand and already she feels the tears stinging her eyes when Maggie finishes up with:

". . . down at Jamaica Hospital."

Velma had never seen anything like it in her life. Needle marks everywhere, blanketing her breasts, around her neck, hidden in the spaces between her fingers and toes. Tracks, up and down the inner and outer parts of her thighs. Her arms were riddled with them and even around the rim of her vagina and on the supple skin of her backside.

Machines, monitors, and tubes hooked up to every limb of Audrey's frail body.

Was this her Audrey Rose? Couldn't be, Audrey Rose hated needles —

Velma looked a bit closer and saw her own cheekbones lurking beneath the sunken, dark spaces beneath Audrey's eyes. There was Chuck's full bottom lip and his mother's eyebrows. But still she couldn't be sure.

"Are you sure it's her?" Velma kept asking the doctors.

Chuck was annoyed. "Of course it is," he'd shot at her over his shoulder. He had Audrey's hand in his, he was whispering to her and wiping at nothing on her forehead and cheek.

There was a tattoo on her leg, right above the knee. A heart, dripping out the name: *Selena*.

"Who the hell is that?" Velma asked.

"How should I know?" Chuck responded.

Velma wouldn't touch her, was scared even to look at her too hard. Suppose she was dreaming? She couldn't stand it if she was, couldn't stay sane waking up another morning to find that it had all been in her mind. She stood against the wall, closest to the door and watched. Let Chuck cry in the shower this time, no, she wouldn't be fooled again.

Someone had found her in the alleyway of an Upper East Side apartment building. Slumped over and gagging for air, a needle close by, the footprints of a fleeing john still visible in the mud.

Respiratory failure. "It's not uncommon in heroin addicts," the young female doctor said.

Velma had just clutched her purse closer to her chest.

Audrey swung in and out of consciousness for eight days while machines breathed for her and liquid food kept her full. Chuck gave blood while Velma cursed herself for not having any scriptures to turn to.

Dr. Joseph, barely five feet, waif-thin with blond hair and Korean eyes, suggested in English heavy with French accents that they (Velma and Chuck) should think about what it is they wanted to do if Audrey's condition did not change in the next week.

What they wanted to do? Chuck didn't seem to understand what it was the doctor was trying to tell them.

Velma understood, though; she felt that familiar crawl beneath her skin that occurred when she saw an animal dead in the road or attended a funeral service.

Lucky enough, Audrey's eyes popped open days later and she sat straight up in bed and asked for a glass of water.

Everything hurt, but worse of all, her stomach felt empty and sour. She looked around and found Velma's face looking back at her. "Where's Selena?"

It had been nearly two years since they'd seen each other. Velma was mother and father to Camilla and these were her first words to her? Velma stood back and bit down on her bottom lip. Selfish bitch, she thought, but instead she said, "No hello or nice to see you, Mom?"

Audrey looked around the room and then back at Velma. "Where she at?"

Velma let go of a little laugh, one just small enough to let Audrey know how ungrateful she thought she was.

"I don't know who the hell you're talking about."

Even after they brought her home, Velma still wasn't sure it was Audrey. Maggie had backed herself all the way up to the wall and even when the heels of her feet knocked up against the floorboard, she still kept trying to shuffle backwards and away from the sight of Audrey. Velma supposed she was trying to shove herself right through the wall.

"Stop it, Maggie," Velma hissed at her as she shooed the gaping questioning little ones away with one hand, while the other was anchored beneath Audrey's armpit.

Together, Chuck and Velma helped her up the stairs and got her settled back into her old bed.

"Who dat?" a wide-eyed Camilla asked one of the other little ones.

"Your mama."

Days stream by like water, Audrey floating along, buoyant in the surf, holding her breath just in case she forgets how to float, she's never known how to swim, but floating has been second nature to her forever.

She doesn't know what's worse, the sour churning feeling in her stomach, or the creepy-crawly things beneath her skin. Sometimes she sees things on the wall, spirits crouching in the corners. She dreams about Selena, craves her during the first few days. Weeks later, she touches her mouth and down between her legs and wonders

143

how in the world she could have done such a thing. She chuckles to herself, but the disgust is there, and soon that burns away to simple embarrassment.

She tries to scratch the tattoo away, but it just scabs and in a week, it's looking right back at her again.

It's days before she can keep down anything but broth. After that they almost go broke buying apple and orange juice and bags of chocolate candy.

Nothing stays quiet. There are no secrets and people who have *heard* or *seen* call up and brazenly ask:

"How's Audrey?"

"How you and Chuck doing?"

"You need some help, anything. Can I bring you something?"

Others call and tell her:

"You get her on that methadone."

"You don't bother with that methadone shit, it's just another goddam drug!"

"Pray."

Someone has a brother strung out on it, another claims that a cousin of theirs is robbing people out near Crossbay Boulevard in order to get money for a fix. Someone admits that a younger sister is turning tricks downtown to stay high and an eight-year-old readily offers the fact that his mother is on the verge of eviction because sticking a needle in her arm is more important than a home for him and his four siblings.

They've all got a story about heroin.

Maggie watches Audrey closely. Watches as she avoids the children, stepping around them like garbage. Hardly ever bowing her head to look down at the young questioning eyes that gaze up at her as she moves through, pretending not to see the thin young arms spread open and waiting for a hug.

Maggie hugs them instead; lifts them up in the air and crushes them against her. She kisses cheeks and lips and mussed and nappy hair and then she looks at Audrey and Audrey pretends not to see her.

Camilla scurries behind her, ducking behind walls, scampering beneath tables and covering her eyes with her hands whenever Audrey does decide to acknowledge her. But it's weeks before she touches her, weeks it seems before she even remembers Camilla is hers.

Velma grits her teeth and waits and gives Audrey space to fall back into place, gives her the time she needs to understand that this is home, this is where the real love is.

Progress is made slowly. Audrey touches Camilla one day. Just a finger to flick away toasted crumbs from around her mouth. A smile follows but little else for a few days. And then there's a conversation about the clouds and the sun. Camilla points at things in the house and calls off the names of the colors. She counts to ten and then sings her botched version of the alphabet song.

She walks on her toes sometimes and Audrey scolds her for that and restrains herself from asking, "Do you want a mustache too?"

Camilla walks on her toes anyway, because she is a willful spirit, just like her mother, just like Velma, she walks on her toes anyway and tells Audrey that she's going to be a ballerina.

They connect for good when Camilla grabs Audrey by the hand one afternoon and leads her into the living room so that they can watch cartoons together.

Velma says, "Go give this to your mother." "Go tell your mother this." "Go tell your mother that," and Camilla knows just whom Velma's referring to.

Months later, Audrey is looking both ways before crossing Rockaway Boulevard, Camilla skipping happily at her side, talking a mile a minute about everything and sometimes breaking out into song — Audrey is aware of how she and Camilla's fingers link together, but little else.

Audrey is caught up in her own thoughts. Thinking about Leroy and well, some of everything else, but especially one thing, well, two, if you count the watermelon.

The watermelon had represented the hazy hot days of summer and the card games of spades and bid whisk that took them late into the night. Velma smiling more than usual and Maggie trying her best not to be too annoying. Everybody on their good behavior. Everybody trying their very best.

Audrey supposed it had to have been the watermelon that had gotten her through, its juicy ruby-pink flesh sweet against her tongue. She would just think of it when the cravings came. She would just think of it and it would be there, waiting in the fridge, a new one cradled in Chuck's arms as he came through the door from work.

It was the watermelon and *not* the love. If she believed *it* was the love, then she would have to believe *in* the love and she believed that there was no room in her heart for a conviction of that magnitude.

"Mommy, Mommy!" Camilla yanks at Audrey's arm, demanding her attention.

"Yes, Camilla?"

Nothing of urgency. Camilla's red mitten has slipped off and onto the ground. Not really rose-red — Audrey muses as she retrieves the mitten and places it back onto Camilla's tiny hand — more watermelon in color than anything else, she decides.

No, no her heart was crowded with watermelon thoughts and visions of Camilla, knelt down in prayer just before bedtime, the feel of her curled into Audrey as she slept, her mouth twitching, small smiles cresting on her lips like waves, riding, riding so long that Audrey would have to bend and kiss them before they disappeared back into Camilla's childhood dreams.

It's November now and the fruit-stand crates are chock-full with pumpkins, yams, and apples; the streets are busy with people hustling from here to there. The sound of their feet, heavy and hooflike in Audrey's ears drown out the *one two buckle my shoe,* Camilla is reciting over and over again. It's November, slate-colored skies and no more watermelon, naked trees, frigid mornings and most days the sun just seeming to wink and vanish.

November and Audrey longing for something other than the comfort and safety of home. Needing more than what Velma can cook and serve up on a platter or dish out in the paragraphs of encouragement she recites like rhetoric every night — more than any amount of bear hugs and *I love you, baby* — Chuck offers, more than Maggie's awkward embraces or the wet kisses and unconditional affection her daughter provides.

Audrey kisses Camilla at the door of her nursery school classroom, wishes her a good day and walks off into the late-autumn sun in search of the *more*, in search of the poppies.

Less than three months have passed and although Audrey is not far from home, she's miles away from her family. Locked in a world of darkness, daylight is just a memory to her. Leroy has her again and the heroin has both of them. He steals and robs to buy it and Audrey dances some nights and others, she works the airport warehouses, inhaling jet fuel while sucking on the dirty dicks of mechanics. She swears they ejaculate oil into her mouth instead of semen.

The Good Reverend Panama gives them a place to sleep in the vestibule of his new temple and sometimes he invites Audrey up to his apartment above the church. He's kind to her and allows her to shower, gives her a free hit of smack and then he takes her. It's violent; he bites her skin and sometimes slaps her face and calls her names.

The sex rattles her and sometimes she opens her eyes and sees Leroy standing at the doorway, smoking, watching, and waiting his turn.

While he's inside of her the Good Reverend Panama whispers, "I am your God." He says, "Say it, say it, Audrey."

Audrey looks him right in the face, but she doesn't see his eyes, crooked nose, or the cross imbedded in his tooth, all she sees is what she knows, what she breathes and lives for, all that's in her eyes are poppies and she responds, "You are my God."

Audrey is close by and she dials her mother's number to listen to Velma's "hello, hello. Who is this?"

Audrey says nothing. Velma presses the phone against her ear and they breathe together until Audrey can't take it anymore and hangs up before she can hear Velma whisper, "Audrey?"

Bobby, Velma's oldest, finally seems to be settling down, getting comfortable in his manhood skin and obtains a job as a night watchman with Four Brothers' Express Shipping. He tells Velma the hours are easy. Midnight to eight, off on Sundays and Mondays. He even gives Velma some money for the kids and brings by a bottle of whiskey on Monday nights for him and Chuck to share and watch football.

He reprimands the children, his kids, for calling him Bobby instead of Daddy and Velma just looks at him, puts her hand up and says, "It's too late for all of that."

He's living with a woman now, someone named Doreen. A dark-skinned girl with big teeth and hips so wide she has to walk sideways down the hall that leads to the living room and Velma has to pop Chuck upside his head to get him to stop grinning like a damn fool.

"Babies?" Doreen repeats like Velma is speaking a foreign language when Velma asks, "You got any babies?"

"No, ma'am. I'm waiting until I get married to start a family."

Velma smiles and nods her head and thinks, Bobby's got a good one this time and then she wonders, how in the world he's going to be able to keep her because Doreen's got two years of college, five years at the telephone company. She drives her own car and the only name on her apartment lease is hers.

Velma looks at Bobby and then Doreen and pours herself a taste of the whiskey and asks, "Bobby, you got gold growing down between your legs now?"

She has to ask, because why else would a woman like Doreen want a man like Bobby?

Doreen blushes and giggles behind her hand while Bobby says, "You know that's right, Mama, you seen it right after the doctors did!" He winks at her and drains the whiskey from his glass.

He's still with Doreen when May rushes in like some newly married virgin anxious to show off everything she's got. The air is stripped of its chill and May throws her head back and spreads her legs and showers the air with the scent of honeysuckle and newly cut grass.

The scent of hickory weaves its way out of grills that are pulled out and set aflame weeks before Memorial Day and Maggie catches Camilla pressing her lips against the fence and stealing kisses from Poe; Pooh bear forgotten on the grass, one button black eye staring up at the clouds.

Women, all in full bloom and expecting in the fall, wobble in and out of local stores, their heads filled with images of green-, yellow-, pink-, and blue-yarned things. Babies born in the dead of winter lay on their backs in carriages, pink-gummed and toothless, barefoot and squirming.

Birds perch and chatter for hours on the telephone lines above the houses, while below them ants construct mounds of earth and march out in lines from between sidewalk cracks.

Spring is loud and warm and joy creeps into the veins of folks that complained the entire winter about heating bills and snow.

Bobby came in late that night. The man he was relieving, a white boy with hunched shoulders who was attending John Jay Criminal College in the daytime and working there at night had just shot him a disgusted look before grabbing his nudie magazine, shoving it into his back pocket and slamming out the door.

"Hey, man, it's just twenty minutes, damn," Bobby yelled at his back before adjusting his hat and hooking the flashlight to his belt.

His eyes red and his head twisted, Bobby couldn't wipe the grin off his face if he tried.

Doreen had come home from work, stripped down to nothing, climbed into the bed and straddled him. He was only half-awake when she shoved him inside of her and started riding him like a racehorse.

His mouth was nasty; gooey nasty from the chips, cheeseburger and beer he'd had before he climbed into bed. His mouth was nasty but she didn't care, she stuck her tongue in it anyway.

Fully awake, he gained control and tossed her off of him, flinging her down to the bed and flipping over so he could mount her from behind.

"All this ass!" he crooned and slapped her massive behind before leaning back on his haunches to watch it tremble.

It was all he could do to contain himself and hurriedly grabbed hold of her waist and positioned himself for entry, but it was too late, a sound caught in his throat and he came all over her back.

"C'mon, Bobby, c'mon, baby stick it in me," Doreen purred and pushed back against him.

Bobby groaned and collapsed on her back, fiddling with her breasts as a type of consolation prize.

"What?" Doreen said and turned her head to look back at him. "What!"

"I'm sorry baby I —"

"Shit," Doreen mumbled and pushed him off of her. "Wipe this shit off my back please," she said, climbing out of the bed. "Now."

It wasn't funny then. But now after the three shots of brandy, he could look back and see the humor in it.

Bobby made his rounds, all the while humming to himself and curling his fingers around the joint he had stuffed in his pants pocket. He would smoke it in the bathroom after the buzz from the brandy faded and then he would snooze for an hour.

There were still some workers there, men who were suppose to be relocating crates to make room for new shipments that would come in the morning. For now, they were seated in the corner of the warehouse, cussing and playing blackjack.

Around two A.M., the women would come through, the prostitutes that worked the warehouses. It was Friday, payday and the four women that usually solicited their bodies would triple to twelve.

Bobby scratched down between his legs and thought that maybe tonight he would join in the fun too.

By 3 A.M., humping and groaning sounds emanated from dark corners and sailed above the large wooden crates. Bobby, content with the three hits he'd taken from the joint, leaned forward and increased the volume on the transistor radio and thought about Doreen.

That only made it worse. His dick, his Johnson, was already stiff and pushing through the blue polyester of his work pants. He'd ordered it down, but it refused to budge. "Beast." Bobby laughed as he caressed it.

He approached the card players. They squinted at him through cigarette smoke. "Yeah?"

Someone cried out from behind one of the crates. Bobby turned toward that direction and grabbed hold of the only weapon they'd provided him with, his flashlight.

"Yeah?" the man said again and set his cigarette down in the ashtray.

They didn't respect Bobby. Not his authority. Certainly not the color of his skin. But it had been all good. Bobby just needed a steady paycheck.

"Just uhm, wanting to know if I could get some action."

The men turned their heads to exchange looks and for split second their faces fell into shadows. "Blackjack?"

Bobby shuffled his feet, but kept his

hands folded at his pelvis. "Nah," Bobby mumbled and nodded toward the groaning moaning sounds.

"Oh," one of the men said. "She be through in a minute."

Bobby stood waiting. He felt like an idiot standing there in his Banter security uniform, hiding his erection.

A man slipped out from the shadows, he was zipping his pants up and grinning. When he sat down, the light caught his brow and Bobby could see that it was covered in sweat.

"Go on." The man threw over his shoulder at Bobby.

Bobby hesitated for a moment. He'd never done anything like this before. Well, not with a prostitute anyway. He'd done it with strangers that were not so unfamiliar after a few words and maybe a drink. This was new to him.

He walked into the shadows.

"What you want, baby?"

The voice was thick and guttural.

"What you need, baby?" It came again, and then the sniffing sound.

"Uhm." Bobby didn't know what to say. He could barely make the woman out in the shadows. The dim light that spilled in over the crates lit on one of her ankles and made its way up to her thigh. It was nice, he thought.

"How much?" Bobby said and took a step further into the darkness.

"Blow jobs five dollars."

Bobby had four dollars on him and a half-smoked joint. "I got three dollars," he said.

There was a sigh and then the sniffling sounds again. "C'mon."

Bobby let the darkness swallow him and he reached out with his hands until he felt hair, forehead and eyelids. She smacked his hands away and then she worked at getting his zipper down.

"Oh, you're so big." Her tone was tired. Bobby imagined that in her line of work she'd uttered those words millions of times.

Bobby put his head back and closed his eyes. His hands found the back of her head and he forced her to swallow him. He could hear himself hitting the back of her throat; he could hear her pulling air through her nose, his own breathing, and his heart beating in his ears.

"Oh, shit, oh shit!" he whispered and coiled his fingers through her hair, guiding her. "Faster, faster," he moaned and felt his knees begin to buckle as his orgasm raced through his body and exploded.

"Oh, oh, oh," he cried as he stroked her hair.

She pushed him away and spat.

"Three dollars," she said and he saw her move away from him.

He wasn't back yet. He was still flying above the crates, small pleasures exploding in his chest and stomach. His penis jerked happily. Bobby smiled.

"Yeah, yeah." He reached into his pocket.

"You got a cigarette?" she asked.

"Yeah." Bobby reached into the breast pocket of his shirt and pulled out a pack of Newports. He shook one out and was just going to hand it to her, but decided to light it first instead.

The flame burned off the shadows and Bobby took that moment to look at the woman who'd just serviced him.

The cigarette dropped from his mouth and when the match stem burned away to nothing, Bobby didn't even feel the flame against his thumb.

When he grabbed hold of Audrey and yanked her to her feet, she slapped him across his face and made an attempt to knee him in his groin. He stumbled backward and knew immediately from the wild look in her eyes that she did not know that he was her brother. He caught her by the throat next and dragged her out from behind the crates and boxes, into the white light and pulled her face to his so that their noses touched.

Still she did not seem to know him and spat in his face and then dragged purple glittered nails across his cheek, before he punched her in the nose and sent her sailing unconscious to the ground.

The men, the card players, watched quietly, before a lone voice asked if she had tried to rip him off. "Most of them are junkies and try to lift your wallet while they're sucking you off," he said.

Velma couldn't seem to get a straight answer from Bobby. She was caught between the sight of her daughter and the blood that crusted on her son's cheek. Her eyes swung wildly between Bobby and Audrey and then she asked for the fifth time, "Where you find her at?"

Bobby was shaking, his hands fumbled with the pack of cigarettes he'd pulled from the breast pocket of his shirt. Smacking it violently against the palm of his hand as he paced the floor, avoiding all of the eyes that stared back at him.

Audrey was spread out on the floor, the children milling around her, whispering and pointing, expertly avoiding Maggie's and

Velma's swatting hands. "Go on now. Git!" they bellowed at them.

"You come on and help me get her upstairs," Chuck ordered Bobby and hooked his hands beneath Audrey's armpits.

Velma started shaking her head slowly back and forth. Her mouth was moving, but no sound came. Bobby, still fidgeting with the pack of cigarettes, his feet planted in the floor, just stared.

"No, no, no." Velma started and backed away from Audrey. "She ain't gonna keep doing this to me. To us," she whispered and her eyes fell on little Camilla, who was peeking out from the dining room.

Chuck's eyes narrowed. "She our child, Velma!"

"Umph!" Maggie sounded.

"We got other children," Velma whispered.

Chuck ignored her. "Boy, get her legs so we can get her up these stairs." Chuck spoke to Bobby and indicated Audrey's legs with his chin.

Bobby still didn't move.

"We can't help her. The kinda help she need we don't got!" Velma's voice climbed to a hysterical pitch and the children grew quiet. Camilla clutched Pooh bear to her chest and felt her bladder open up.

161

Velma looked around at the wide-eyed faces and slowly, gently, took the pack of cigarettes from Bobby's hand. She shook one out for him and one for herself.

Bobby took the cigarette from Velma and slid it between his lips. He fumbled through his pants pockets before finding his lighter and igniting the tip of his cigarette and then leaned over and did the same for Velma.

They inhaled together and Bobby seemed to regain some small part of himself. Maggie moved to the couch and sat down. "I can't have her here. Not again." Velma spoke to the carpeted floor, the curling cigarette smoke and then finally Chuck. "I can't do it again," she said and leaned back into the couch.

Camilla Rose

Poe is her first friend and second love after Tom Jones.

He is an eye, an ear, and a lip. Fragmented Poe parts with a voice. Camilla knows his fingers though, those he manages to poke through the fence slats.

She is five and he is six.

Camilla falls in love with him as they share bags of candy and bites of peanut brittle. She allows him to lick her ice pops and laughs when he sticks the iced cherry-red tip of his tongue back through for another taste.

Right there alongside Maggie's collard greens and the tomatoes Velma has decided to grow, Camilla's five-year-old heart leaps about in her chest when Poe tells her he will grow up to be Batman and she will be his Catwoman.

Poe "is sickly," his mother Joan explains to Chuck and Velma a week after they move in next door. "An only child," the mother spouts. "Lord knows, I don't need no more. Taking care of him is a full-time job."

Velma smells the beer on her breath, takes a step backward, and smiles. The father, Arthur, is jolly. He's round, short, and bald and forgets to let go of Chuck's hand after they shake. "Poe ain't sickly, she just smothering is all. He's a boy, let 'em be a boy!" Arthur booms and slaps Chuck hard on the back.

Poe sees the front of his new home only on his daily comings and goings to school and even then the sight of it is obstructed by his mother's large hips and beefy arms that she folds across her massive breasts. His time in the front is brief; the yellow school bus is always on time.

On the weekends when school is out and teenagers invade the schoolyard and take advantage of the basketball and handball courts, Poe is relegated to the backyard, and the wooden clubhouse his uncle built for him, his only company, most times, are his maroon-colored bike and blue ball.

He talks to himself during those warm daylight hours and makes smashing and bombing noises with his mouth as he manipulates his plastic toy soldiers in a childhood game of war.

He is lonely. Camilla sees the loneliness swimming in the eye he presses to the gate when she and her brood of cousins come slamming out of the house and into the yard to rip and run and play pretend. They don't always know he's there, because he doesn't say a word and his eye blends in with the brown centers of the dwarfed sunflowers that grow along the fence.

Sometimes even Camilla forgets about him. We forget about the people we love sometimes.

There were things that baffled them.

Simple curiosities that had to do with the sun, the moon, thunder, snow, and Santa Claus. She and Poe contemplate these great mysteries in their adjoining backyards. They discussed it in small voices, scrutinized the facts, as only little children can; their sentences running long and brilliant like a string of pearls. Their voices rose and dove and leveled out to short silences while Camilla adjusted the dress of her Barbie doll and Poe did some annoying boyish thing.

Camilla wondered just exactly who this "Man" was that was keeping everybody down, especially her Uncle Bobby. It was all he could talk about when he came to visit, tilting his beer bottle up to his mouth with one hand, and balancing his Newport cigarette between the fingers of his other. " 'The Man' don't want to see me get no-where," he'd complain.

Sometimes Chuck would nod his head in agreement, other times, though, he would grab up a newspaper and fling it at him. "Find a damn job!"

Bobby would just huff and curl his arms around Velma's waist, kiss her neck and whisper in her ear. "Just lend me twenty, Mama; I'll give it back to you next week."

Velma would sneak him the money at the door when she hugged him good-bye, knowing that it would be weeks, maybe months before she saw her son again, pockets empty and nothing more to offer her except his company and complaints.

Uncle Sam was another one that didn't seem to have any good intentions. Well, Camilla certainly didn't care for him; she heard Chuck say that Uncle Sam always took half of his paycheck and how he'd read in the newspaper that Uncle Sam was going to raise taxes . . . again.

Camilla wondered why this Uncle Sam never came to visit, never called, and never ever showed up on Christmas Day with a gift for her. He did, however, send letters, letters that Velma and Chuck always seemed to argue about.

166

The most baffling of all to Camilla was the talk about crackers. Those crackers this and those crackers that. Crackers had done a lot of bad things to black people from what Camilla could understand and so she wanted nothing else to do with them and refused them even when Maggie took the time to smear them with peanut butter and jelly.

The white lady was another problem. The white lady, Chuck complained, "Just won't let Audrey go."

The white lady, Velma said, "Had a lot of people hooked and messed up. She got all three of Lucille's kids."

"If Audrey got off that white lady, maybe she could get herself together and come on back home," Chuck said quietly, and Velma nodded her head in agreement.

The summer Retha came to spend with them Camilla was six years old and had never seen an albino. Great-Aunt Retha, tall and pale, with kinky blond hair she wore braided in two thick plaits, rolled and pinned above her ears so that the tiny sapphire earrings she wore were always visible.

Her eyes were a pale gray and her lips, a dim pink. Retha's arms were long and sinewy and Camilla wondered how the wooden bracelets she wore didn't just slip right off her wrist. Retha made clicking sounds with her mouth but Camilla had seen her refuse every stick of gum ever offered to her.

Camilla observed this strange-looking woman from the safety of Maggie's hip. "Who she?" Camilla whispered into the green material of Maggie's housedress.

"What?" Maggie said and tried to shake Camilla loose with a quick snap of her hip.

Camilla hung on and then pinched the flabby skin of Maggie's waist. "Who that?" she whispered again after Maggie tugged lightly on one of her pigtails.

"Her?" Maggie tilted her chin at Retha. "You know who that is."

"She the white lady, right?"

Maggie chuckled as she peeled Camilla's tiny fingers from the material of her housedress. "I suppose she is."

"She the one got my mommy all hung up, so she can't come home?"

Maggie stopped and looked down at the child. "What?"

"The white lady, every one messed up, 'cause of her," Camilla said.

Maggie didn't know what to make of what the six-year-old was babbling about.

"She ain't got your mama. That there is my mama's sister. She ain't got your mama," Maggie said and finally succeeded in undoing the child from her hip.

Camilla was exposed now. Maggie had left her standing alone in the middle of the living room, all eyes were on her. Camilla covered her face with her hands.

"She's a cute something, ain't she," Retha commented before raising the delicate teacup to her lips again. "She looks just like Audrey, don't she?" she said, that clicking noise sounding between each word.

Velma smiled sadly and nodded her head.

"Come on over and give your Great-Aunt Retha a kiss, Camilla," Retha urged and held her hand out to Camilla.

Camilla squinted at her through splayed fingers, shook her head *no* and moved as quickly as her skinny legs would take her, up the stairs.

Retha stayed with them for a month, and during that time, things were said in front of Camilla that her young mind could not comprehend. Words that sounded menacing to Camilla, words like *cancer* and *doctors* and *chemotherapy* and *mastectomy*.

The adults' voices would rise and soar when they talked about this thing called remission. When Velma talked about remission, her voice would take on the jubilance it did when she talked about cards, parties, and summertime.

Camilla had heard one of her cousins whispering about Aunt Retha not having any tits. "Not one, they chopped them both off with a kitchen knife," one said.

"Doctors don't use kitchen knives, they use scalpels, stupid," the other responded.

"That's why she ain't got no husband, 'cause she ain't got no tits. No man don't want a woman without any tits."

"Who told you that?"

"I heard Grandpa telling it to Mr. Head who was here asking 'bout her."

"Mr. Head was asking 'bout who?"

"Aunt Retha."

"Her husband died eight years ago, that's why she ain't got no husband, not because she don't have no tits."

"He died after they cut 'em off."

"You lying."

"Ain't."

Camilla sat close by digesting all of it, but not understanding any of it. She went into the bathroom, raised her shirt and examined the small brown spots on her chest. She would have tits one day, Velma had told her so. "Nice big ones too." She'd laughed and cupped her own breasts. "Just like your

170

grandma." She smiled. "Just like your mama."

The sadness struck abruptly, like lightning, unexpected and out of place in the middle of a calm summer evening. Velma's smile slipped from her lips and her shoulders curled forward, and she seemed to wither right there in front of Camilla.

Velma heaved then, not to exhale breath, but to discharge the misery that thoughts of Audrey brought on.

The air in the room was suddenly heavy and even after Velma walked off, Camilla still found it hard to breathe.

Retha caught her in the bathroom, sitting on the toilet, her small scrawny legs dangling, Leroy's sharp knees, jutting, the rounded rubber heels of her sneakers knocking against the pristine white porcelain throat of the toilet.

She had her hands down between her legs, rubbing herself, poking at the pointed flesh, getting some enjoyment from it but not as much as the wad of Bazooka Joe bubble gum she was munching on.

She couldn't get her hands up fast enough when the door swung open and the gum tumbled right out of her mouth and landed on her lap when she looked up and straight into Retha's gray eyes.

" 'Scuse," Retha said and started to leave, but then didn't and her right foot fell on the black-and-white ceramic floor. "What you doing, little miss?" she asked, stepping fully into the bathroom and pulling the door shut behind her.

Camilla could feel the air leaving her lungs. She could hear it escaping as it whistled in her ears. Red heat crept across her face; she was dying, she was sure of it.

She folded her hands and looked down at the sticky wad of gum that mocked her from her lap.

The summer sun spilled through the window, coating Retha in white light that washed her pale complexion clear.

Camilla chanced a glance at her and then dropped her eyes again.

"You oughtn' be messing with your stuff down there," Retha said as she turned and primped in the large oval mirror that hung over the sink. "You'll catch a disease," she said and ran her pink tongue over her pink lips.

Camilla said nothing.

"Go on and get up now. You done finished your business." Retha smiled a bit and sighed before finishing. "Or whatever it was you were doing."

"You ain't gonna tell no one, are you?"

Camilla said in a hushed voice. She couldn't stand the ridicule from the other children or the lash from Velma's heavy hand.

Retha smiled, "No. I won't tell. It'll be our little secret."

Satisfied, Camilla climbed down off the bowl and pulled her panties and shorts up around her waist, before turning to flush the toilet.

"You forgot to wipe, honey," Retha said as she started toward the door. Camilla, embarrassment cloaking her once again, raised her hands to her mouth, a nervous gesture she'd developed over the years, and then dropped them suddenly when the stink of herself rose up from her fingertips. "But I didn't do nuthin'," she whispered.

Retha chuckled again, before turning to give herself one last look in the mirror. She touched the rolled plaits above her ears and then ran her index finger over her blond eyebrows, before smoothing out her billowing blouse and that's when Camilla saw it, the nothingness beneath the blouse.

Retha was all flat, no tits. It was true.

"She a lady, ain't she?" Camilla quizzed Maggie again.

"Yes."

"You sure now?"

Maggie scooped out some peanut butter with a spoon and stuck it in her mouth. She nodded her head *yes*.

"Ladies have tits, don't they?"

Maggie opened her mouth to show Camilla the glob of peanut butter and saliva on her tongue. Camilla jerked her head back and made a face. "That's nasty, Maggie. Quit it!" she yelled.

"Ladies have tits, right?" Camilla urged.

Maggie smacked at the peanut butter for a while as she tooled the spoon around the jar.

"Grandma said you weren't to eat out of the jar like that," Camilla reminded her as she wedged her middle finger down alongside the spoon and pulled out her own glob of peanut butter.

"Ladies have tits. Yes," Maggie said and stuffed another spoonful of peanut butter in her mouth.

"How come Aunt Retha don't have none, then?"

Camilla watched Maggie as she worked at the peanut butter in her mouth. She swallowed and mumbled something before turning her attention back to the jar.

"What? What you say, Maggie?" Camilla yelped and grabbed at Maggie's wrist.

"I said, they cut 'em off 'cause the cancer

had got in 'em," Maggie growled before shaking her wrists free.

There was that word again.

"What's cancer?" Camilla asks, but Maggie says nothing else.

Retha's time with them is over. Her brown suitcase and shopping bag filled with New York things are sitting by the door. The sun has just begun to climb into the blue morning dissolving the last vestiges of the purple night. Velma stands over the stove and stares at the steam billowing from the kettle's spout.

Her mind is on Audrey, always on Audrey now and she picks at the dry skin of her cuticles, peels away at a scab on the back of her hand, anything to chip away at those thoughts that keep her welded and staring at nothing.

She seems restless, standing there pouring water into teacups and dumping instant coffee in one, a tea bag into the other. Wiping her hands against her apron, then dragging her fingers through her hair and sighing, always sighing. But she offers a smile to little Camilla who comes slowly down the stairs, sleep-crusted and yellow in the corners of her eyes, her Pooh bear, ragged and dirty, clutched in her arms.

"You up early, baby," Velma says and grabs a mug from the cabinet. "You want some hot chocolate?"

Camilla shakes her head *no*.

"Why you up so early?"

Camilla just shrugs her shoulders.

Velma considers her for a while and then eases herself into one of the dining room chairs. Camilla moves to the couch and curls herself into a ball.

Retha comes down from the bathroom just as Velma blows cool air across the top of her teacup.

"Mornin'," Retha says to Velma. Velma nods her head and tests the tea with the tip of her tongue. Camilla leaps up and folds her legs Indian-style beneath her. She clutches Pooh bear to her chest and rests her chin on his head, but she doesn't speak.

"I made you some coffee," Velma says and indicates the cup across from her. "You want some breakfast? Eggs, grits?"

Retha shakes her head *no*. "Coffee just fine for now."

"You should eat something. You got a long bus ride ahead of you."

"Too early to eat so heavy. The coffee is just fine," Retha says and pulls up a chair.

They sit in silence until Camilla creeps in and positions herself at Retha's elbow. She has to know. The bags are at the door and sun rays are curling like fingers around the drawn shades and casting golden slants across the floor. Time is running. She needs to know if it's true. She has to know.

Camilla touches Retha's arm.

"Yes, baby?" Retha turns her head and lays soft gray eyes on Camilla. The clicking sounds follow and then the faint pink-lipped smile.

"Can I see?" Camilla whispers and her eyes move to Velma's confused expression and then back to Retha's gray eyes.

"See what, baby?" Retha says and turns her body all the way around.

"What you wanna see, child?" Velma sets her teacup down and leans forward.

Camilla can't say it, so she just points to Retha's chest.

Velma gasps and shakes her head, "Camilla!" she shouts and slaps her palms down on the table. "You take your little fresh behind right up —"

Retha raises her hand, bringing Velma's anger to a halt. Her smile doesn't waver and the gray in her eyes turns powder soft.

"You sure you want to see?"

Camilla nods her head *yes*.

"Now, Retha, you don't have to —" Velma begins again, but Retha just shakes her hand and Velma shuts up for good.

Retha slowly undoes the clear buttons of her white blouse and pulls the material apart. She has on a T-shirt, similar to Camilla's own. Delicate straps, with a tiny pink flower at the center of the neckline.

There are bumps pushing through the cotton material, but no tits. Camilla squints at them.

"You sure now?" Retha says before she grabs the hem of the T-shirt and begins to roll it between her fingers.

Camilla's mouth drops open and her tongue turns to paper as she nods her head *yes* again. Pooh bear's black-button eyes seem to bulge as Camilla's grip goes tight around his neck.

Retha's stomach is soft-looking and creased. The sun ignites the fine white hairs there and Camilla thinks of the dust that rests on everything wooden in that house.

Retha rolls the material and her smile wavers a bit, the clicking sounds come faster and faster until the shirt is up around her neck and Camilla is staring at twisted knobs of scarred flesh.

Velma groans and Camilla can't move. Her knees quake, but her feet won't go even though her mind has demanded them to run, run!

It lasts longer in her mind than it actually does. Retha's T-shirt is down and blouse buttoned, by the time Camilla feels as if she can breathe again.

"Okay?" Retha says and cocks her head to one side.

Camilla nods her head and blinks. The taste is coming back to her mouth and she loosens her grip on Pooh.

Retha smiles and clicks and then she leans in and asks, "Do you have any questions?"

Camilla nods her head, ignoring Velma's menacing glare, leans in and asks, "Will they grow back?"

Retha smiles and responds. "Yes. In heaven. They will grow back in heaven."

What she remembers on that last day of childhood was her sitting alone on the stoop of her grandparents' home, Pooh bear and Barbie dolls a distant memory and buried somewhere in the attic or down in the basement among the other remnants of time long gone and Camilla, twelve years tall with pressed hair, always worrying Velma about getting a relaxer and training bra.

She puts more time into smearing Vaseline on her knobby knees and sharp elbows than schoolwork or the dinner dishes that became her chore after Doris and Fleet got grown enough to decide that they'd rather live with their mother.

Camilla had thought less and less of Audrey by the time she spotted her strolling towards her.

She remembered not knowing what to do with herself, her hands or even how to fix her mouth when Audrey started across the street and then stopped in mid-gait to gaze at something shiny in the road.

It had been just six months since Audrey's last visit. That one had gone horribly wrong. Audrey had gotten away with the VCR and three of Chuck's power tools.

Velma, screaming her head off as she chased Audrey around and around the dining room table with a butcher knife. When she caught her, Camilla had the terrible sense that this time, this time Velma would do what she'd been threatening to do for years. "I brought you in this world and I can take you out!" But instead, she whacked Audrey across the calf with the flat side of the knife before grabbing her by the collar and dragging her to the front door.

Audrey started towards her again, right hand up over her head, fingers treading the air and Camilla's mouth going dry with fright or excitement, she didn't know which, and then a nervous smile skirted her lips and to her surprise she found her own hand up in the air waving back.

Twelve years old and still clasping hold of that unconditional emotion that only children possess and how unbelievable it seemed that after all Audrey had done — Camilla still craved her presence, still felt a jealous need to be close to her.

It was Christmas in September and Camilla's heart fluttered inside of her chest as she watched her mother move steadily towards her. An easy smile resting on Audrey's lips and Camilla thinking that wasn't really walking, not the one-foot-in-front-of-the-other–type of walk; no, Audrey had a swagger that moved her left to right, snakelike.

"Hey, baby!" she yelled, arms stretched out like wings. "You too big to give your mama some sugar?"

Closer now, Camilla sees Audrey's skin is speckled with dark blotches, teeth, not so white, one missing, hair curled under mushroom-style, the uneven ends beating against her cheeks as she comes.

"Camilla, c'mon now," she sings even though she's still a whole house away.

Camilla felt her body lift and her hands were suddenly wrapped around the tops of the egg-shaped poles of the fence.

She should call for Velma. Someone grown. But Camilla is still a child after all, and she wants Audrey all to herself, without the questions and the crooked looks.

"Mama," she whispers and is suddenly embraced by wire-thin arms, her head pressed tight against bone and deflated balloons of flesh where full breasts should be and the rank scent of the forgotten and destitute clogging her nostrils.

Camilla wanted to snatch away from her, but Audrey held fast and they rock for three summer–drenched minutes, while neighbors pass, point, and smile.

When Audrey finally lets Camilla go, she steps back and drinks her in. "You sure do look like me," Audrey comments. Her words are like molasses; they slowly drip from between her lips and drop in globs at Camilla's feet.

Audrey offers a sleepy smile and with one long finger absentmindedly flicks Camilla's greasy bangs away from her eyes.

Camilla notes the dirty fingernails and the gray smudge of filth on her palm.

"You all grown up now, huh?" Camilla nods. "Your grandmama home?" Audrey asks, looking at the house for the first time.

"Yes," Camilla responds.

Audrey nods her head and pushes her

hands into the back pockets of her jeans as she rocks on the heels of her shoes. "Oh," she mumbles but does not make a move towards the stairs.

"You want me to get her?" Camilla asks.

"Hmmmmm." It wasn't an answer, just a slow churning sound in Audrey's throat. Her eyes moved to Camilla's shiny almost-new ten-speed. "This yours?" she exclaimed and ran her hand along the curl of the handlebars. Camilla nodded her head *yes*.

"You ride?" Audrey asks, her eyebrows reaching for her forehead, the dullness in her eyes suddenly dissipating.

"Yep," Camilla proudly announced and poked out her budding breasts.

Audrey chanced a glance at the house again. "Lemme see," she exclaimed and clasped her hands together. "Down to the corner and back," she whispered, before her tongue toyed with the empty space in her gum.

Camilla mounted the bike and maneuvered out the gate and onto the sidewalk. She took a breath and pushed off. She was flying. Camilla knew every bump and valley in that sidewalk. Had ridden over it a million times and now she rode for Audrey, her mother.

Camilla's bangs lifted and hung in the wind as she pedaled her way past Mrs. Logan's grinning face and Fannie Birdsong's gardening-gloved hand. She raised her chin and inhaled summer's bouquet and when she reached the corner, she tilted the bike left and allowed the back tire to skid across the pavement.

Audrey stood at the gate, clapping, her eyes dancing and her mouth cheering for her daughter, Camilla Rose!

She beckoned Camilla back to her and she came swiftly, the wind tearing her eyes, her legs pumping, feet pedaling, pedaling until she was almost upon her and thought, briefly, that she could run Audrey down right then and there and be done with her for good.

But she was twelve years old and as much as she hated her, she loved her more and brought the bike to an abrupt and screeching halt. The edge of the wheel kissed the rounded toe of Audrey's dirty sneaker.

"Oh, Camilla!" she squealed and reached out and touched her cheek. "You're so good. Real good."

Camilla, she just grinned.

"Can I try?" Audrey said and her eyes shifted to the watching faces of the neighbors, to the blank and staring white screen door of the house.

"Uh-huh." Camilla vigorously nodded her head up and down. She was so eager to please her, this woman who had left her countless times.

Audrey eased one shaky leg over the body of the bike and then positioned herself on the seat. Camilla saw then that the jeans sagged, how there was more material than flesh.

Audrey started out wobbly. The bike swayed and tilted, threatening to fall, but then she remembered her childhood, and she steadied the bike and began to pedal. Her knees pumping, pumping until she was at the corner and turning. She was confident by the time she whisked past Camilla the third time, her behind above the seat and her chin jutting outward, cutting through the soft summer air.

Camilla put her hand out as Audrey tore past her the fourth time, her fingers brushing against the emerald green of her T-shirt. "Last time, I promise!" Audrey yelled out at her, and Camilla nodded her head in the way she'd seen Velma do a million times when Camilla or one of the others begged for one more cookie, a glass of Coke, or just to stay up past bedtime.

She nodded her head and folded her arms across her tiny bosom. It was such an adult demonstration, she felt grown and leaned her hip against the fence and watched as Audrey Rose sped down to the corner and took it.

She waited for her return and when she saw Velma's face looking out at her from behind the screen of the storm door, and realized that the sun had taken on that fiery orange of evening, she knew Audrey would not be coming back. Not that day or any of the days that would follow. She would be gone again for a good long while. Just like last time, just like always.

Velma pushed the door open. "Camilla, time to come in now." She almost let the door slam shut and then Camilla could see that something in her mind clicked and she caught the edge of the door just before it bounces on the jam. She pushed the door back on its hinges and her eyes swept the street and then settled on Camilla. "Where's your bike?"

Years trail behind Camilla's departing childhood as it sulks away into the nothingness of yesterdays, leaving Camilla in the here and now, always in the here and now, while Audrey comes and goes like autumn leaves, winter snow, licorice-colored tulips, and summer. Audrey is temporary, but Camilla is resilient.

Children are like rubber bands, Velma reminds herself when she confuses the hatred in Camilla's eyes with disappointment — she finds comfort in this defense, no matter how thin it is, it provides the belief that whatever damage done is temporary, like its inflicter.

But that is a lie. The hate is seeded.

Camilla's thirteenth summer and Audrey is holed up on the gloomy second floor of an abandoned Bronx tenement preparing to lose herself, while in Queens jaybirds sing and caterpillars inch their way along garden walls as Poe leans in and gives Camilla something to refer to years later when life suddenly spins out of control.

His family is moving south and Poe has come to say good-bye.

Their lips brush, and then press together just as Audrey uses her index and middle fingers to wake the vein in her right arm.

Poe and Camilla wrapped in morning sunlight, pressed close to each other, glowing coals in the pits of their stomachs and the sound of rushing water in their ears. They mistake the sound for rushing water, not experienced enough to understand that it's blood sprinting through their veins.

Poe and Camilla not knowing what to do after the kiss and before the final good-bye and so they just smile at each other as Audrey's head lolls on her neck, the needle forgotten and at attention in her arm. She succumbs to her own tide. She smiles too.

When Camilla turned fourteen she began to lose bits and pieces of herself traveling between home and school and back again, while her mother misplaced every bit of her sanity crossing the waters between Staten Island and Manhattan.

The sea was calm, flat as glass, yet Audrey lurched about the deck of the ferry as though enmeshed in a great storm.

Wild-eyed, matted hair, and orange-colored lipstick applied perfectly to her bloated lips, Audrey bumped into nearly twenty people as she zigzagged her way towards the ferry's bow.

She grabbed hold of the arm of a burly-looking gentleman who promptly snatched away and then shoved his meaty fist into her face.

She whispered, "Won't you help a sista out?" to a dark-skinned woman who snuffed at her before grabbing hold of the hand of her Asian boyfriend.

Audrey could clearly see the murky blue water that seemed to be rising up to meet her. In her mind, Aretha Franklin belted out "River's Invitation" and that's when she tossed herself into a group of schoolgirls who squealed and scattered.

Catching hold of a baby carriage, "Hold on!" she screamed at the stunned young mother who seemed to be able to do little else than stand stock-still and wide-mouthed.

"Don't you see it!" Audrey screamed as she dragged the stroller along. The infant, just about a year old, nodded her head and it was then that Audrey knew for sure that she hadn't totally lost her mind, but that it was somewhere on the ferry and the cleaning crew would be sure to find it and return it to her when this whole mess was done.

Some Good Samaritan jumped out from the crowd and snatched the stroller from Audrey's grip; another leapt forward and tackled her to the ground.

"Thank you," Audrey whispered hoarsely into the wood-plank floor. "Thank you."

"Strings?" the young white male officer

questions for the third time. "Strings, wrapped around your arms and legs, trying to pull you into the sea?"

"No. Ropes. Maybe they were vines?" Audrey mumbles as she looks wildly about her.

"Whoa," the manly looking female officer barks into the air and then twirls her index finger at her temple. "This one is out of the park," she adds before letting off a long whistle and then pointing to the track marks on Audrey's arm.

"The baby saw it too," Audrey says before they ease her into the back of the police car. "Ask the baby."

"I live with my grandparents," Camilla hears herself tell Amanda Smiley on her fourth day at Madam Vivian's College Preparatory School. "Both of my parents are dead," her mouth lies just before Mr. Contreras, the Spanish teacher, sulks into class.

"An orphan."

The fable makes its rounds.

"No parents? Not even one?" Liz Beth Collins questions and then comes close to tears when the answer is, "not a one".

It's during fifth-period lunch, just before Thanksgiving. Cardboard cutouts of turkeys, pumpkins, and colored corn on the cob taped to hall and classroom walls, there are even bales of hay stacked fashionably outside of the school's entrance. It's there, over the squash bisque and French bread that lay waiting on the orange food tray that Amanda, twisting the end of her blond ponytail, giggled her way through a story about a boy with, "The dreamiest eyes you ever did want to see!"

After that, Joanna Perkins shared and Camilla learned that she had the hots for Julio. "The stable boy?!" Meredith Marshall screamed. (They're students at the same riding academy.)

Joanna goes pink with embarrassment and then a fiery red.

"He's Mexican, isn't he?" Amanda whispers her question like *Mexican* is dirty word.

"Did he sneak over the border?"

"I dunno." Joanna shrugs her shoulders.

"He is illegal though, isn't he?"

"I guess so. Aren't they all?" Joanna poses the question to Camilla like the color of her skin makes her an expert on these matters. They all turn and wait expectantly for Camilla's response.

Camilla looked into the blue, green, and brown eyes of her pale-skinned, pink-lipped, narrow-waisted schoolmates and cocked her head thoughtfully to one side.

Camilla, just one of two blacks in the 240 all-female student body — the other was Lequisha Baumbry, who was coal-colored and smelled like Posner's hairdress. Pint-sized, but muscled, Vaseline-faced Lequisha wore cheap gold rings on every finger and had two holes (that currently held thread thin strands of straw) bored in each of her earlobes.

Lequisha Baumbry was on scholarship just like Camilla but holding down an after-school weekend job on top of maintaining a B+ average; in order to help out at home and someone said, "To take care the baby she'd had over the summer."

Camilla didn't know how true that was. But Lequisha seemed to care less about her fellow students, preferring to sit alone every lunch period bouncing her head to the music that streamed out of the earphones of her Walkman, seemingly engrossed in what-ever Donald Goines novel she happened to be reading.

Lequisha was "too black" and her "ghetto attitude" intimidated them and so they flocked to Camilla, the golden-colored one, for all of their inquiries.

"Can I touch your hair?"

"Do you wash it every day?"

"Do you tan?"

"We eat a lot of steak and potatoes in my house, do you eat a lot of fried chicken?"

"Are black boys' dicks really as big as I've heard?"

Camilla, not wanting to be delegated to the far side of the lunchroom, but more flattered by the attention, happily answered each and every question.

Fifteen years old and a sophomore in high school, bombarded with images and schooled with people that have her unhappy with her nose, the space between her eyes and the fact that her hair is just long enough to brush the nape of her neck and no matter the strength of the relaxer; in six weeks or less, Camilla's wavy roots would be pushing back through her scalp again to remind her.

Camilla can't find anything good in the shape of her lips or the double crescent moons her behind imparts in the seat of her jeans and so she begins to strip away her blackness by using a penknife to carve petals from between her thighs. She knows that there is white meat beneath her brown skin.

That lasts for a month and ends when Velma asks about the pin-sized spots of blood that dot Camilla's bedsheets.

★ ★ ★

It was there as if waiting just for Camilla or maybe suddenly decided against by some other confused girl who panicked and left it behind.

White top blinding against the gray of the counter, looking awkward alongside the bottle of Buckley's and the blue tube of denture cream Camilla had been sent to buy.

"And this too?" the young male cashier asked in a disinterested voice as he picked it up and twirled it around in search of the sticker price.

The label stated: *Queen of the Nile Fade Cream*.

"Yes," Camilla said.

The first few nights she rubbed some on her knees and then sat staring at them until the wee hours of the morning. She yawned all through English class and decided she would try some on her wrist, where the skin was lighter and she supposed, easier to fade.

She called herself all kinds of names the next morning when Velma had to practically drag her out of the bed. "Stupid," she muttered as she brushed her teeth. The label promised results in just seven to ten days, not seven to ten hours!

She wanted so much to be like them. Them who seemed to have everything and want for nothing. Not one tale was told that involved addiction. They all had their mothers and most had their fathers every other weekend, four days during Christmas and Easter break and three weeks in the summer.

Not one, from what Camilla had heard, had ever had to cook a meal on a hot plate because the gas bill hadn't been paid or had had to send an uncle out into the cold to offer the Con Edison man a ten spot and stiff drink to forget that he was sent to that particular house because the occupants were sixty days past due on paying their bill and there weren't going to be any more final-notice letters; just him sent out with a lock and instructions to cut those non-paying Negroes' electricity right off!

And she was doubly sure that those girls had never eaten mayonnaise sandwiches for Saturday lunch, sat down to a pancake dinner, or had to add water to stretch the milk for a bowl of cereal.

Sweet sixteen for the girls at preparatory school meant nose jobs, European holidays, and new cars.

Camilla asks for Velma to consider these things for her sixteenth birthday but all Velma considers is Camilla over the rim of her new spectacles and says, "Have you lost your ever-loving mind, child?" before laughing and asking Maggie if she heard what Camilla had asked. Of course she had, she was sitting right there. They laugh together and Velma turns her attention back to her television show.

"Well, can I get a weave then?"

"No," Velma says shortly without pulling her gaze from the television. Camilla watches her for a while. "Why?" she says and Velma's eyes roll behind her lenses. "Because I said so," she snaps and then her head spins around so fast that Camilla thinks it will make a full 360-degree rotation before it comes to a stop.

"Don't start thinking you one of them W's you go to school with." Velma spits and then looks at Maggie and says, "Camilla forgetting who she is and where she come from."

Maggie nods her head and then blankets Camilla with an empty gaze.

"Don't forget who you are, Camilla," Velma reminds her and then sends her off with the wave of her hand.

Too late.

She can't sit still in her chair. Twice the teacher throws her a strained look, but Camilla can't stop fidgeting. Even in the dark, she feels the eyes on her. The projector, just a row behind her, makes clicking sounds that say, "nigger, nigger, nigger," as it unfurls the film.

The announcer says, "People in Third World countries all over the globe are starving."

Africa must be the world, Camilla thinks, even though it looks like the smallest continent on the atlas and in her world history text.

They all look like her and her family.

There is poor crippled Maggie scooping up dirty water for drinking, a barefoot Velma walking with a baby strapped to her back, one growing inside of her belly, basket of fruit on top of her head. Camilla blinks and sees herself, guiding Audrey through alleyways thick with refuse.

In social studies they talk about inner-city crime. "Bring in examples of this on Thursday," the teacher instructs and the students bring in newspaper clippings of black boys, shot dead in the street. "Drugs," the teacher spits, "is a big problem in the ghetto, well, that and welfare." And the blue, green, and not-so-dark-brown eyes fall on Camilla.

February. Black history month. Frederick Douglass, Martin Luther King, Rosa Parks. Every February, all of the same names, all of the same information. It seemed to Camilla that the black race was all out of heroes.

At assembly, Mrs. MacDougal leads them in a chorus of: "We Shall Overcome."

In English class, Mr. Abraham assigns *Black Boy*.

Camilla's sixteenth birthday finally arrives and she knows that Clorox only burns the skin and does not bleach it. Velma bakes her yellow cake with white frosting, perches a pink-and-red *sweet 16* candle on its top. The traditional happy birthday song is sung, followed by the Stevie Wonder version.

They eat fried chicken and French fries and Doris calls to see if Camilla got the sweater she sent her and there's the ten-dollar bill in a envelope from her Uncle Bobby with *This is all I could spare,* and a smiley face scrawled on the flap.

"I baked the cake!" Maggie snorts and turns her head when Camilla looks her way.

Avon products and a subscription to *Jet* magazine and then Chuck presents her with a birthday card while Velma stands smiling proudly at his side.

"Fifty dollars," he whispers proudly in her ear.

Camilla says thank you, kisses cheeks, makes a wish, blows out the candle, has a slice of birthday cake and two cups of grape soda before saying good night. Spring and summer. Autumn and leaves falling and Camilla still poor and black and confused.

Christmas and secret-Santa time at school and Claudette Bell catches her in the bathroom and asks, "Would you change names with me?"

"What?"

Claudette pulls her into one of the stalls. "You see," she begins, but Camilla is lost in Claudette's milk-colored skin and she can see, even before the braces are removed, that Claudette will have perfectly-straight teeth and as fashionable as the glasses are that she wears now, Camilla knows that they will be gone next term, replaced with colored contacts — "I got Lequisha and well, you know how she is, well, she's . . ."

Claudette seemed stuck for words so Camilla uttered the internationally acknowledged, "Yeah," making it easier on the both of them.

Claudette perked up, "Oh, Camilla, I'm

so glad you get it," she said and burst out of the stall. "So who will I be Kris Kringle to now?" Claudette sang as she stood in front of the mirror checking her teeth and smoothing her chestnut hair back into place.

Christmas cards decorate the banister and the house becomes alive again with the holidays. People drop in with bottles of liquor and fruitcake, Chuck dusts off his seventy-eights and speaks intelligently about Ella Fitzgerald's riffing while the men bop their heads and snap their fingers, sometimes they pull air between their teeth like something smarts, but Camilla hears someone say, "That was sweet, wasn't it?" and Chuck lifts the needle and moves it back a few grooves on the vinyl so that they could all experience it again.

In the middle of Camilla listening hard and trying even harder to understand the "sweet" of the music — word comes that Leroy Brown is dead.

Velma listens intently, pressing the receiver against her ear, nodding her head and then finally saying, "Yes. Thank you."

Velma calls her into the dining room, offers her some tea, "Would you like some eggnog or spiced cider?" She fiddles with the aqua-colored material of her blouse, focuses on the plate of Christmas-tree cookies resting on the table, before easing herself down into the chair.

Camilla waits through the moments that Velma tries to find the right words, and reaches for a cookie.

Velma rises again, takes stock of the filth that has settled on the slats of the window blinds and then finally her focus settles on Camilla again.

"Leroy is dead," Velma spouts and braces herself for the flood of emotion. Camilla blinks. "Who?" she says, spraying bits of green sugar and baked dough.

"Leroy, your father," Velma says and finally sits down, clasping her hands together and resting her elbows on top of her thighs.

Camilla smirks and thinks, *one down and one to go*. "Oh," she manages to utter and digs deep down inside of her herself, finding a pitiful piece of something Audrey left behind; placing it on her face she is able to fool Velma into believing that she is woeful.

Leroy Brown, not even forty, but looking years beyond that and dressed in a pair of Lee's and blindingly white Adidas sneakers, with a black T-shirt covered with green-and-red graffiti art that depicted a marijuana leaf, a gun, a syringe and a bottle of Olde English beer. White casket, blood-red lining.

Camilla looked down into his withered face and didn't know how she was supposed to feel. He had been her father, but he had never been her daddy.

Not even his mother, Tonya, had been a fixture in her life. Camilla had been in her company six, maybe seven, times since she was born.

Now Tonya, wracked with grief and slumped over in the front pew, suddenly jumped up and hollered, "They shot him, they shot him dead!"

Velma's eyes bulged and mouth collapsed, providing Camilla with a clear view of the ball of spearmint gum that rested comfortably at the center of her tongue.

No one had shot Leroy Brown, but there was a smoking gun and that was the filthy hypodermic needle that had infected him.

Camilla looking restless and bothered all of the time. Despising everyone who lives in that house, not a civil word to share with any of them. Her responses to their inquiries come in the form of exasperated bursts of breath, neck rolls, and eyeballs that rotate on cue in their sockets.

She has an after-school job at McDonald's.

Pocket change that Velma believes, will keep Camilla in movie and pizza money, but instead Camilla spends her earnings on eyeliner, Lee press-on nails, and pony hair that she pins to the top of her head bestowing herself with a *Jeannie*-esque quality.

"You look like a whore," Maggie says matter-of-factly one day. "That lipstick is too loud for a girl your age," Velma adds after one glance. "Perfume just as loud."

"And cheap," Maggie adds.

Camilla storms out, the dozens of Boy George and Prince buttons pinned to the gray men's blazer she's wearing as a fall coat this year, makes a racket as she goes.

Seventeen is upon her and three letters of acceptance to prestigious colleges come in the mail, two with offers of full scholarships. The family celebrates with twist-top wine and Pink Champale — that's not really champagne, but Camilla knows that they don't know any better.

May and senior prom and Liz Beth offers up her brother as a date for Camilla. Cody, a junior at West Point.

"Her parents are dead. A murder-suicide. I think her father was a pimp or something like that," Liz Beth explains. "I just feel sorry for her. I mean it's not like she's a dog or anything. . . ."

Cody was not the bleeding-heart liberal his sister was. "Yeah, real sad," he mumbled and then stuck his palm out for the twenty dollars that went along with the favor.

Audrey sits shivering on the green bench. A late-May moon above her head and Central Park sprawled out behind her. Joggers, cyclists, and strolling police officers here and there, the need bad, and veins on fire, her pockets even empty of lint.

Her eyes roll in her head and her body slides left as she feels the safety of sleep taking her or maybe this time even death, but then her belly burns empty, while the rest of her body screams for a fix and her muddled mind happy to have either food or drugs begins to chant, "Choose, choose, choose."

Audrey snaps erect again, wipes at the spittle swinging from her bottom lip as groups of young people decked out and smiling, hugged up in the back of horse-drawn carriages, or jutting out of the tops of limos, corrupt her view.

Colorful corsages pinned to taffeta-covered bosoms or wringing wrists hurt her eyes and the scent of alcohol and perfume swirl through the air around her and Audrey, eager to look at something other than the tiny painful flowers, focuses on the looks that pass between the clean-cut boys and understands immediately that the smiles they toss over the shoulders of their dates have to do with the condoms that they've tucked discreetly into the compartments of their billfolds.

Their only concern is sinking into the wetness and maybe hearing the snap of the hymen and on Monday being able to point a finger and push out their chests and say, "See her, I popped her cherry."

Audrey sees all of this and Camilla sees her and hears Audrey's mouth say "Beautiful!" and then "Can you spare some change?"

Some drop change, others make space. Camilla turns her head away but Cody, Cody spits right in her face.

It wasn't her.
Camilla tries to convince herself.
Just someone who looked like her.
She toys with the probability.
The eyes were definitely hers. Mine. Velma's

*and Maggie's and who knew how many other
Roses before.*

She thinks.

Audrey's eyes float in behind Camilla's
squeezed-shut eyelids, rattling her concen-
tration, allowing unpleasantness to seep in
where pleasure should be: Cody's kisses,
the needy words he whispers in her ear.

Tears clog her throat and she opens her
mouth wider, Cody tastes salt.

Those eyes spin in her mind. They are
stunned and then hurt. Camilla opens her
eyes and hopes that Cody does not see the
tears.

She kisses him harder.

Why didn't she laugh? Hadn't it been
funny? They had all laughed and pointed
and jeered after what Cody had done.
Maybe if Camilla had laughed too, Audrey's eyes wouldn't be haunting her.

In the back of his father's Cutlass, Cody
pins Camilla's arms over her head, re-
straining her like he's had to take every
piece of ass he'd ever had. He wrestles with
her slip and then struggles with the hooks of
her bra.

The prom dress, a simple light-blue
sheath made special by the white-feathered
collar; that he tugs roughly up over her

head. Camilla looks up and sees Audrey's eyes pinned to the felt ceiling above her head. She squeezes her eyes shut again and parts her legs.

It's over before he expects it to be and before Camilla realizes it's even begun.

"Black girls are so hot," Cody mutters in her ear and gives her one last thrust for good measure. Camilla's head bounces against the car door.

"You on something, right?"

"What?"

"The pill?"

"No."

"But this is your first time, right?"

"Yeah."

"Good, you can't get pregnant your first time."

"Oh."

Cody eases himself out from between her legs and reaches into the front seat for his pants. Camilla scoots up and searches the floor for her stockings while her panties dangle tragically from the ankle of her left foot.

She leans back into the seat, thrusting herself into a jagged frame of moonlight that suddenly illuminates her skin.

"Damn," Cody moans as he squints at

Camilla's breasts. "Is that some type of rash?" he asks and then has to resist the urge to scrape his tongue against his teeth.

"No," Camilla says as she carefully pulls the dress down and over her milk-white breasts. "It's a skin condition."

She remembers quite well the last time she saw them. November 16, 1988. Camilla was eighteen years old.

Velma seated at the table, her hair pulled back into a tattered ponytail, the gray at her hairline just beginning to show. There was a green tin ashtray before her, a burning cigarette resting at its center, smoke curling up and over her head, stretching in to lace and then vanishing into the walls. She had offered Camilla a strained smile before she tilted her head and allowed Camilla to press her lips against her cheek.

Velma had winced, like Camilla's kiss had pained her.

High school graduation just three months behind her and most of her life packed away in three suitcases and four small boxes. Not much of anything left in her bedroom, just some old records, dog-eared textbooks, a picture of her and Poe Scotch-taped to the large oval mirror, a note from an admirer folded in four and forgotten in the blue-

and-yellow keepsake box, a battered pair of sneakers, and three or four articles of faddish tops that hung huddled in the corner of her closet; not much of anything that would even make them feel like she would be coming back.

She was not one of them, had never been, God had made a terrible mistake by placing her with them and now she was going to make everything right again.

Camilla had chosen to attend Smith College and had decided on majoring in journalism. "Like newspaper writing?" Maggie inquired with awe.

She said she would take the train, that a taxi could drop her at Penn Station and she would manage from there and no, no she wouldn't have it any other way and then with a whip of nastiness, "Could you finally just do *one* thing I want you to do without giving me a hard time about it?"

Camilla made her way to over to Maggie who was wedged tight into the corner of the sofa, her arms crossed tightly across her breasts, face screwed up into some type of emotion neither Chuck nor Velma could read.

"I'll see you for Thanksgiving," Camilla lied.

Maggie had just shrugged Camilla's hand off of her shoulder and continued staring at the television.

Chuck was standing at the door with an anxious look on his face. His eyes swinging frantically between Camilla and the taxi that sat humming at the curb.

She remembered how his fingers worked at each other, quick and snakelike and the fact that he'd decided to let his beard grow in, the chaffing brush of it against her cheek when he pulled her to him, hugging and kissing her like it would be the last time he'd see her.

She remembered it all.

The Present

Camilla Rose

By the time Bryant finds the lump Camilla is grown and so far away from that life that it almost seems as if it didn't exist at all.

Married, four years now, and living in Scotch Plains, New Jersey.

Split-level home, inground pool, cedar deck, picket fence, and two luxury vehicles in their three-car garage.

Four bedrooms, all furnished. A family room, living room, dining room complete with crystal chandelier, and solid oak table that could be extended to seat twelve instead of eight, whenever she cared to.

A kitchen with frostfree refrigerator and six-burner stove and more cabinets than she knows what to do with and even when Camilla does give Lena a day off and decides to prepare a meal, she never thinks of ham hocks and collard greens, egg noodles, and chicken wings. Her oven has never baked a pan of cornbread, her broiler never used to toast bread, not ever.

She is a journalist; well, a columnist,

really. Dear Rose. She helps people with their problems.

A local celebrity, she can't even go to the supermarket without being recognized.

"Are you Dear Rose? Well, that ole picture does you no justice!"

White and black write to her. It's true; the photo that sits at the beginning of the column does her little justice and leaves her ethnicity up in the air.

On sight, though, it's apparent. "She's just clear," the Caribbean women who live on Front Street, comment. "Red," the Trinidadian men say. "More beige than anything else." Tulsa Grand, who had been greeting visitors at the reception desk of the *Union County Times* for more than forty years, remarks.

Bryant Boston. Another one you had to look twice at and then still think. There was something about Spanish and Belgian ancestry. His mother, Babette, claimed to be two-quarters Creek and reared in Savannah — claimed to have been christened Babette, but Camilla saw a legal document that named her Babe-Ann, born in Nutbush, Tennessee.

She married all white men after Bryant's father left her for her distant, younger cousin Nora Mae. After that, Babette paid good money to "close up shop" as she put it and had the doctor tie and burn her tubes. "Black men," she was found of saying, "always want you to have their babies. White men, well, they just wanted to have you."

Camilla met them in Vermont.

She'd spent one semester at Smith and then transferred the following spring to Bennington College after presenting the financial aid office with two death certificates (fakes obtained via mail for fifty dollars). Her legal guardians had been killed in a tragic fire and she was on her own now. "Please send any correspondence to P.O. Box . . ."

She was waiting tables at a small restaurant in Stowe. Bryant and his family were seated at her station and he'd been smitten immediately. Camilla with her doe-shaped eyes and button nose. She had a soft round chin and Maggie's dimples etched into each cheek. Although he was a breast man, he still found quiet satisfaction in Camilla's slim waist and generous hips.

Bryant was immediately impressed by Camilla's calm and pleasant demeanor and the fact that she didn't flinch, not once, even when Babette returned her soup for the third time.

Afterwards, he'd slipped her a fifty while his family gathered themselves to leave. A fifty, with his name and number scrawled across Grant's face.

That was in '95.

They kept in touch by phone and after some time he came to visit and she spent the summer of '96 with him and his family at their Victorian home in Cape May. The ring came the following Christmas and the wedding May of '98.

He didn't stir much of anything in her, but she supposed that wasn't important. She had been searching for a particular sort of man. A white man at first, but then when she could find none that would have her as his wife, she began setting her sights on Latinos and lighter-skinned men of color.

Addiction-free and no illegitimate children, she wanted a man from the right side of the tracks and she found that in Bryant.

Early on in their relationship he'd asked about her family. Camilla hadn't decided what lie was appropriate and so had danced around the subject, taking him by the hand and guiding him elsewhere to her lips, her breasts, down between her legs.

But on their fourth date, which happened to be a family dinner, and after watching the Discovery Channel the night before, Camilla suddenly decided what she would say.

"My parents are dead." It had slipped quickly and over the foie gras and stuffed quail. Babette's eyes had gone saucer wide as she struggled to keep the wine she'd just sipped inside of her mouth. "A skiing accident, near the Himalayas, I think, I was young. Just three years old."

The lie was out and hanging in the air between them.

"Oh, Camilla," Bryant breathed and the love that had begun to grow swam in his eyes.

"Dear child. I'm so sorry to hear that," Babette said and reached over to touch Camilla's wrist.

Bryant knew that Camilla's grandmother had raised her, but not much else.

"So you were raised by?" Babette inquired before dabbing the corners of her mouth with her napkin and leaning in.

"My grandparents, until I was seven and then Grandpa passed on, leaving me and Grandmama alone."

Babette cocked her head. Grandmama, was she serious?

"After I graduated college," Camilla continued, proud of the story she'd come up with on the whim, "Grandmama fell in love with an African lawyer, moved to Ethiopia with him, and is now working beside him with the dissidents."

It was as simple as that. A few grand tales, a couple a hundred jars of fade cream and *poof,* that house, her color and those people just vanished.

Now Dr. Franklin's question had made them all real again.

Camilla felt her throat close up.

"Camilla?"

"Y-yes, doctor?"

"Does your family have a history of breast cancer?"

"No, not that I know of."

Dr. Franklin said there were other ways to get at it now. She didn't have to be cut in order for them to do the biopsy. There were new procedures; something called an ultrasound-guided core biopsy. "A needle that is inserted directly into the mass," he explained. "We'll numb the area, of course, you won't feel a thing. It'll all be fine. I'm sure you don't have anything to worry about. It'll all be fine."

He kept saying that, kept reassuring her, but Camilla didn't feel like it was all going to be fine.

"Friday," Dr. Franklin had said. The Band-Aids the nurse put over the pinholes the needle had made in both breasts, snatched at the silk of her bra cup. "We'll have the result back next week Friday," he said.

Camilla's eyes shifted and she clutched her handbag tighter.

"Maybe less," Dr. Franklin added and shuffled some papers in her file.

But her heart seemed to know something different, seemed to beat irregular now, sounding like Maggie's awkward footfalls, like Poe's ball when he missed it on the come back from the wall, sounding like the old pipes behind the walls of that house during winter when the water struggled to get through.

"Okay," Camilla said and got up to leave.

A week. Seven days, but not enough hours to fill the time.

The green tips of tulips peep out from the dark earth and the birds are already gathering stray bits of string, straw, twig and the white fluffs of stuffing that made its escape from the old couch just before the sanitation truck could haul it away from in front of the Van Courtland house.

Zola is almost a year old and sleeps through the night and only cries when she's hungry or wet. The family room is done and the deck has been retreated and Camilla's anticipation of summer is marred by the threat of cancer.

"Hey girl!" Margot's voice chimes across the telephone lines.

"Hey," Camilla responds dryly, already sorry she picked up.

"I'm coming your way this weekend. Me and a friend." Margot drops her voice seductively and a giggle follows. "A new friend," she adds and then more giggles ensue.

Margot Hilliard, Camilla's partial link to an obscure past. Margot's history was as contrived as her own.

Margot had provided Camilla with an obscene introduction to dormitory life when she walked in on Margot and some boy on top of her. They were both buck naked and Camilla had stood stunned and staring at the smiling crack of the boy's pink behind.

Up on his knees and deep inside of her, the bottoms of his feet were dirty and the strength in his thighs strained as he moved himself up and onto his elbows.

Margot's fingers gripped his shoulders so firmly that Camilla thought the boy's skin would pierce.

Camilla tried to move something, her feet, her eyes, anything, but her body refused to obey.

No noise except their breathing and the cries of the bedsprings and oh yes, something soft coming off the radio.

Tangerine-colored walls glowing beneath the candlelight, boxes still packed and sealed tight, scattered here and there. A life-size poster of a half-naked Prince taped to the ceiling and them, wrapped up so tight, they seemed to be one being.

He breathes a question and Camilla finds herself cocking her head, straining to hear. And then there is Margot's savage, "Yes!" before her legs come up to embrace his back, her ankles lock together and her toes curl under and still Camilla cannot move.

She was fascinated with Margot Hilliard from the beginning.

Margot with her wild curly hair and traces of Russian ancestry in the thin line of her nose. She was the exact color Camilla had been striving for. A more au lait with a hint of café.

They lay there panting for a moment,

before Margot turned her head and caught sight of Camilla in the bureau mirror. "Oh," was all she said and then gently tried to push the boy up off of her. All he did was moan and then she slapped him upside the head and said, "Get the fuck off of me!"

"Bitch," the boy said when he finally rolled off. He barely paid Camilla any attention, didn't seem to mind that his balls dangled like Christmas bells between his legs for all the world to see as he searched the floor for his clothing.

Margot draped herself in a red Chinese silk robe, but did not knot the belt; making herself comfortable at the edge of her bed, she promptly crossed her legs.

"Where you from?"

Margot didn't need to know Camilla's name, not just yet, she just needed to know if this girl standing in front of her was from anywhere close to where she was running from.

"Queens, New York," Camilla said and stepped out of the path of the retreating boy.

Margot lets go a sound. "He's the chemistry professor's son, you know," Margot spat. "A lot a good it will do me," she says finally, pulling the panels of the robe together. "It's the father I should have been

222

banging," Margot breathes and then looks down at her perfectly polished toes. "Queens, huh?"

The first time Bryant met Margot, was on his wedding day.

Bryant and Babette had forgotten to smile and close their mouths when Camilla and Margot started towards them, hands linked and grinning. There was a moment when Babette could safely exchange a questioning glance with her son, but it was just a moment and then the waiter sidestepped and there she was again in a dress so short, heels so high, and breasts so big that Babette forgot to make a mental note about the horrid color of her lipstick.

Camilla had told him that she and Margot were the "best*est* of friends."

And that was true, because only a best friend could overlook the shallow misgivings of her Hollywood-bound comrade — while the other ignored the fact that her gal pal became lighter-complexioned with each passing year.

Bryant's eyes shifted to the pile of delicate crystal tableware nearby and it would be a number of years before he would remember exactly why on first seeing Margot, he'd suddenly thought of dessert plates.

Margot sails into town on the back of bad news with her new beau in tow.

Lars, lovely, lean, and Swedish with hair so blond it looks white. Thin-lipped with perfect teeth and eyes so blue, Camilla has to hold her breath whenever she looks into them.

Bryant is amused by him and when he and Margot are alone in the kitchen, he catches her by the elbow and shakes his finger in her face. "Traitor," he whispers.

Margot grunts and then smirks before letting out one of her theatrical laughs, swatting Bryant on the behind and mumbling, "All the good black men are taken," she says and then adds, "That also goes for the men that are barely black. *You* of all people should know that."

Camilla smiles through Friday night and Saturday, the secret eating at her as she serves food, laughs, and offers more wine.

Sunday is a blessing. Five more days to go.

Margot has left and the house is empty again. Camilla notices the ticking sounds of three clocks in three different rooms of the house. She hears the humming of the dishwasher, the whirling sound of Zola's animal mobile and her own beating heart. She concentrates on these sounds, hunts them down and silences them.

Wednesday and Camilla's jeans are sagging at the waist, her hair dry and brittle at the ends, eyes puffed and swollen and she has started rubbing the heels of her hands together all of the time, just for the movement, just for the feel and comfort it gave her.

"What are you doing?"

Bryant is tired. His eyes are bloodshot. Camilla breaks his sleep at night and this new thing she does with her hands is irritating and worse yet, she won't even compensate for her short attention span or her unkept appearance by rolling over and spreading her legs for him. He touches her thigh and she goes stiff, he climbs on top of her anyway and kisses her mouth and she begins to weep.

"Dammit, Camilla, what the hell is wrong with you?"

Friday at five and Bryant has called to say he will be late and Dr. Franklin's office closes at six, but Camilla is too afraid to call and no news usually means good news, but not always, not in Camilla's world.

"Dr. Franklin is at the hospital today. He'll be in tomorrow. May I take a message?"

Camilla stumbles and can't find her words.

"Is this an emergency?"

"Yes." *Yes* was easy.

"May I take your name and number? I can have him paged."

The words tumble out and the phone is in the cradle again and Camilla stands there and stares at the cream color of it and waits for an hour and rubs the heels of her hands raw.

At eight her hopes are dashed and her legs are weak, feet bottoms burning and Zola is down for the night and Lena wants to know, "Would you like some tea before I turn in?"

Camilla shakes her head *no*.

Eleven o'clock and Audrey Hepburn is on the big screen television, a glass of untouched water is on the sofa table and Camilla is topless, staring at her breast, trying to see the problem, wondering if she's infected Zola or even Bryant; they both loved them so.

Eleven o'clock and the phone is ringing and Camilla wonders why Audrey Hepburn doesn't pick up and then she realizes that the phone is ringing in real time.

"Hello?"

"Camilla, I'm sorry. Is it too late?"

"Who is this?"

"Dr. Franklin."

Camilla covers her exposed breast like he's there, as close to her as the water glass.

"Oh, uhm, yes?"

"Well, the tests are in, but I've been at the hospital all day so I haven't seen them. Would you like to come in tomorrow and we could go over them together?"

"Yes, of course, that's fine. What time?"

"Is eleven o'clock good for you?"

"Certainly."

"Okay, then. Again, I'm sorry about the hour."

"Good night, Doctor."

"Good night, Camilla."

Bryant didn't know what to say when he picked her up. He looked at her breasts first before he looked into her eyes and Camilla believed that she started hating him right then and there.

He had flowers, but didn't know how to offer them to her, so he just tucked them under his arm and tried to lift her from the chair by her shoulders.

The other women in the waiting room watched the scene from over the tops of the magazines they pretended to read. One woman stared blatantly.

Dr. Franklin came out just as Bryant got Camilla to the door and mumbled something in Bryant's ear, before patting him heartily on the back.

The ride home was silent. Camilla staring out the window, and pulling the petals off the flowers, her skirt was littered with them by the time they pulled into the driveway.

"Can I get you something?" Bryant said as Camilla started up the staircase.

"Some water?"

Camilla said nothing and thought what a fool he was. What was water going to do for malignancies?

"Cancer?"

Camilla nods her head. She feels the familiar sting of tears and then her chest begins to heave. She's surprised that there is an emotion left in her body. Every day there are tears, there are hours of anger and long moments of pity and then those desperate minutes of regret, when she takes Bryant's hand and starts to say, "There are some things you need to know." He waits with an uneasy patience and then all she does is cry again and he holds her and pats her back like she's an acquaintance that needs reassuring, not his wife.

"Did you get another opinion?" Margot breathes from California.

"Wasn't any time."

"Can't they just take the part that has the cancer?" she says matter-of-factly.

"It's too risky to leave any tissue behind." It is a mechanical response. Not even her own voice, but that of Dr. Franklin's. "Too risky to leave any tissue behind."

"I'm so sorry, Camilla."

Bryant doesn't know how to ask her, or even if it's the right thing to do. It's just a request really. One last look. He doesn't have to touch them, well, unless she wants him to.

They watch a movie in the bedroom. Zola between them, they try to make things as normal as possible.

Camilla's eyes are on the screen, but he can tell her mind is a million miles away.

Later, Bryant is restless. He thinks they should make love at least. He reaches out for her breasts but his conscience reroutes his hand and it falls on her shoulder. "You okay?"

Camilla smiles and nods her head. "Fine."

A doctor, white-masked and knit-capped, hands covered with plastic gloves and the examination light huge and moon-like over his head. He was grinning, actually smiling behind that white mask of his. She was sure of it; she could see the impression of his teeth through the thin white material.

She squirmed and her butt made an offensive sound against the metal of the operating table. Where was the sheet? There should be a sheet beneath her and she opened her mouth to tell the doctor so, but no words came out even though she could feel her lips flapping against her gums. Her gums? Where were her teeth?

"Fell out along with the hair." The answer seemed to float from nowhere.

Camilla moved her hand up to her head and sure enough, she was bald.

The doctor's head turned left and nodded and then turned right and someone handed him a butcher knife, the light fastened onto the sharp edge of the blade and Camilla squinted against the brightness that jumped off of it and into her eyes.

"Anesthesia!" the doctor demanded as he examined the blade.

Another gloved hand, no face, just a white-jacketed arm and beige rubber fingers holding a Bazooka Joe.

"Open please."

Camilla doesn't want to but her mouth

drops open on command and the rubber fingers release the gum. It bounces off of Camilla's gums and lands on the back of her tongue. Her air is cut off and replaced with sugary sweetness.

"Chew, please."

And she does. The air comes back.

"Ready?" the doctor asks and steps forward, blocking out the light.

"Ready!" a voice sings from the grayness.

"Ready, Camilla?" He grins.

Ready for what? Camilla thinks.

The doctor raises the butcher knife into the air and then brings it down hard onto her chest. There is no pain, just a squishy sound and then the thump of something hitting the ground.

Camilla chews faster.

He raises the butcher knife again and she sees blood dripping from the blade.

"Ready!" he screams.

"Ready, Doctor!" the fairy voice repeats and the doctor brings the blade down for the second time. Another squish and thump.

"All done, Camilla. You can sit up now," the doctor says and backs away from the table.

Camilla sits up. Her eyes find her toes first, then her shins, calves, thighs. The triangular tangle of dark hair, her belly button, stomach and then the open and bleeding spaces where her breasts used to be.

She opens her mouth to scream, but blows a huge pink bubble instead.

The anesthesia slipped away, and the dream right along with it. A dull thumping pain began on the left side of her chest and marched across to the right side.

Bryant was there, seated at her bedside, his focus on something across the room. Every now and again Camilla could make out lip movement and head gestures.

Camilla felt as if she was in a vat of water; her ears were clogged and she had the strange sensation of floating.

Her eyes moved slowly away from Bryant and onto the beige walls, the mounted television a framed painting of purple-and-blue-vased flowers.

She caught the honey-blond streaked curls, the large owl-like eyes, a gold hoop dangling from the right nostril now. That was new, Camilla thought.

"Camilla?" Margot's words came across hushed and thin. "She's coming to, I think."

Bryant was suddenly leaning over her, his face smiling down into hers, his teeth suddenly looking bigger, sinister.

"Baby?"

Camilla moved her lips, but only a dry crackle escaped from her throat.

He was touching her cheek; she felt the stiffness of his fingers, the coldness lodged in his digits.

"Don't, don't try to speak." His eyes went to Margot and then back to her. "The doctor said the surgery went very well. It was a success."

Camilla's eyes rolled in her head. It went well, it was a success. What did that mean? Did that mean they got all of the cancer and that the new seeds they planted in its place would sprout breasts next spring?

What did they know?

Camilla knew that breasts only grew back in heaven.

She can't move her arms. They're just rigid sticks at her sides. Bryant looks at her and sees a walking corpse. Camilla's lips are drawn, her skin sallow. She's weak and depressed. "Well, that's to be expected, Bryant," Babette says.

This is not what he signed on for. Well, did he? He remembers the "Will you take this woman . . ." and of course the "I do." But had he really committed himself to the "through sickness and health" part of it?

Over a stiff vodka he ponders these things and thinks about a woman named Janice who had loved him fiercely once upon a time and he had been stupid enough not to have appreciated it. "I chose the wrong one, Paul," Bryant slurs to the bartender.

Days go by and Bryant makes himself less and less visible. What is there for him to do? He can't help with the changing of the bandages. The room smells like the hospital ward his grandfather rotted away in. The smell reminds him of death. His hands begin to shake.

He can't even be in the room for more than five minutes at a time and so Lena does everything for Camilla while he lurks outside the bedroom door, pacing, feeling ashamed, but feeling more afraid than anything else.

Lena Crass, "a godsend," to hear Babette tell it. Lena came into their lives like a gentle breeze, suddenly and without notice, cognac-colored hands that remind Camilla of the overstuffed brown leather chair in Bryant's office, ring finger graced with a simple gold wedding band from a husband who had been in the ground for fourteen years.

She would describe herself in one word, "committed."

An out-of-work housekeeper and nursing school dropout looking for day work. Calm even though she was running late — gopher-like as she popped her head through the door just as the last interviewee, confident, tall, and European, strutted out.

"So sorry for being late," Lena said without introducing herself as she pushed a creased and somewhat weathered résumé at them.

Wrinkled trench coat soaked through from the rain, Lena remains on the colorful mat that sits at the front door as she undoes the straps of the plastic rain scarf on her head.

Lena Crass, barely five feet tall with a dimpled face and perfectly cut bangs.

Camilla suspects the bun at the back of her head is horse or maybe mule, but certainly not Korean.

She is round like a snowman and Bryant doubts, as he takes her coat, that she won't be able to do much without becoming winded.

"Nice to meet 'cha," Lena says and places her free hand over Camilla's when they shake hands.

Lena has a twang, something southern that brings to mind church bells, peach cobbler, perspiring glass pitchers filled with lemonade set out on a steamy summer day.

They move to the dining room.

"I'm from Georgia," Lena answers when Camilla inquires.

"Oh," Camilla moans softly.

"You expectin' I see," Lena says and nods her chin at Camilla's swollen belly.

"Yes. In December."

"Christmas baby?"

"Just before," Camilla says.

"Two of my boys were born on Christmas day, a year apart," Lena says as her eyes roam around the dining room. "Nice color. Cozy," Lena comments.

"Yes," Camilla agrees.

"So," Bryant abruptly interrupted. "You've been doing domestic work for thirty years?"

Domestic came out cheap, his tone was chafing and Camilla shifted uncomfortably in her chair.

"Yes," Lena says and runs her hand over the polished oak of the dining room table. "I was with the same family for twenty-two of those years."

"Uh-huh, I see that," Bryant says. "Why did you leave them?"

"Well, the kids grew up and the parents died."

"Sorry," Bryant mumbles.

"No need to be sorry, that's life."

"And the Hamptons?" Bryant asks, tapping the name on the paper with the edge of his Waterford pen.

"Oh, they moved out of state. I couldn't go with them, all of my people are right here in New Jersey." Lena stares at one of the wall hangings for a while. "They offered me a heck of a lotta money to go, but I couldn't leave my family," she says more to herself than to Bryant.

Camilla feels ashamed, she left hers.

The wall hanging seems intriguing to Lena and Camilla focuses on it just as intensely, wanting to see just what it is Lena has found so interesting.

"I suppose I understand that," Bryant said.

"Well, family is precious," Lena says.

"Nothing greater, 'cept God." Camilla whispers and pats her stomach.

Lena nods her head in agreement and smiles.

"What was that, Camilla?" Bryant asks, still focusing on the résumé.

Camilla hides her surprise with a small cough. Her mind has not run on that philosophy for years, but there it was tumbling out her mouth like she referenced it every day.

"Nothing," she says.

★ ★ ★

Camilla is in limbo, floating between the pain and the euphoria of the painkillers, her body is pliable and Lena is able to ease Camilla up into a sitting position without causing her too much discomfort.

She loosens the ties that are at the back of the green hospital gown and gently shifts the gown down Camilla's shoulders and then arms, until it falls onto Camilla's lap.

The stark whiteness of the bandage is marred by the large blotches of blood. Camilla breathes in as Lena uses the delicate cuticle scissors to cut through the netting.

She wants Lena to say ready, set, go, or something that would prepare her for what was to come next, but Lena didn't and before Camilla realized it, the bandages were on the floor and she was six years old again staring at Aunt Retha's twisted bits of flesh, except hers were still raw and pink and she could see the crooked stitch the black thread made through her flesh.

"Oh, God," Camilla mumbled.

She supposed she had it coming. And why wouldn't God take from her what she had treasured most. Her breasts. The part of her she had made perfect first by making them white.

It had been her magic armor protecting her from the plights of being born black. Life had moved along smoothly when she started applying the cream to her breasts and had only gotten better with each piece of anatomy she included. By the time she met Bryant, her whole body was four shades lighter and she was eons ahead of where her foremothers had been at her age.

And now that the breasts were gone she thought more and more about Queens and that house and those people. She wondered, as she balanced on the brink of death, if any of them had died and who, if any, would be there to greet her on the other side should she not make it through.

Two weeks after the operation Camilla begins her treatments. "There will be twenty triple-dose chemotherapy treatments of Adriamycin, Cytoxan, and 5FU. Every other Thursday from twelve to five," the young oncologist says.

First treatment and Camilla can't leave the bed for three days.

Second treatment takes her hair.

Third, her dignity goes out the window when she breaks down and cries like a baby two hours in.

Fifth treatment and the veins collapse in

her arms. Bryant moves into the spare bedroom.

Lena drives her most all of the time and never complains about the sick that Camilla almost always leaves in the plastic bag on the backseat.

Weariness settles itself in black half-moons beneath her eyes, making itself comfortable in her spine and in the inhale and exhale of her breath. These days, just raising her hand to wipe at her eye or reach out for her child, fatigues her. She is sure death is on her tail because her dreams take place in pitiless places that are filled with nothing but dark alleyways and broken street lamps.

People huddle hungry and cold in doorways while garbage, caught and coiled in the mouth of the wind, spin at their feet.

Gargoyles sit like pigeons on wrought-iron fences, watching her with their stony eyes as they rustle their wings in welcome and fill the everlasting night with the sound of stone against sandpaper.

Fear is riding Camilla's shoulder and every eyeless person that shuffles past her looks like a family member she's buried in that mass cemetery called her past.

And when she is not asleep, Camilla is in a

perpetual grip of panic, unsure if her lies are true or her truths lies and she weeps for that little black girl she abandoned whose spirit was broken by a mother whose spirit was weakened by a man and his drug.

No matter what Audrey had been or done, she'd been and done it black.

Not poor Camilla, though. She had looked in the mirror a million times and only saw the brown of her skin and not the magic flowing beneath it.

Camilla so busy trying to get white, trying to get right and away from those people and that house, that she missed out on the adoring looks the brothers threw her way or how the sisters watched her every move and studied the rhythm her hips swung to when she walked the block.

Curled up in bed at night, those girls tried to dream themselves tall like her.

Camilla, despised and coveted and not because she was black or the child of an addict or born out of wedlock or living in a house with a cripple who got down on her knees and kissed a bloodstain in the carpet good night — but because she was Camilla Rose, much prettier than her mother and as smart as a whip. "Camilla Rose," her people were heard to say, "had potential and she gonna make something outta herself."

And she had, she'd made a damn fool out of herself.

Six months into the sickness, Lena decides she can no longer smile at Bryant anymore, nor can she smile *with* him, either.

There's been talk at the supermarket, in the house-goods aisle, over select cuts of meat, and out in the parking lot where she and the other live-ins load groceries into car trunks on Thursday afternoons. And even with a week's worth of laundry waiting for them, and schoolchildren to collect, they start the engines and steal a few leisurely moments to whisper about whose doing who's wife or husband in the neighborhood and Bryant's name is fresh meat on every wagging tongue.

"Never thought I'd see him fall from grace," one comments.

"They all do," Lena reminds them before slamming the trunk of the Audi wagon.

Some kind of normal was what Camilla was hoping for on that first day out alone in public. The blue-and-white scarf worn beneath a Yankee baseball cap had sufficed for playtime with Zola in the backyard, but today amidst grown people, she would have to wear one of the five wigs Margot had sent her from Hollywood. The wig and the mastectomy bra. Thirty-six DD.

Normal is all she can hope for.

A peck on the cheek from Bryant and now the customary, "Don't wait up," that he throws over his shoulder as he hurries out the door to work.

A kiss from Zola, instructions for dinner passed on to Lena, and Camilla is off to the office, driving herself for the first time in months.

It's just a small, "Look, I survived this," visit.

That day is not easy and far from normal.

Camilla does not have her magical armor anymore and feels the difference as soon as she steps off of the elevator.

Strained smiles and those pitifully whispered voices that are used around the dead and mourning.

The men are the worst, they look at her artificial bosom first and then her eyes and immediately she is reminded of the coward husband she has at home.

Confusion is a flashing neon sign on male faces and they hum, "W-wellll," while their minds work at the information: Both breasts, right? They'd sent flowers. It was Camilla Rose, wasn't it?

"It's good to see you back," they say

before rushing off to some imaginary meeting or luncheon.

The women are women about it. Connected and concerned, but unaware that they are even treading near offensive as they absently cup one of their own breasts with one hand while the other rests sympathetically on Camilla's shoulder.

"Thank you," Camilla whispers after they share their stories of hope, recovery and survival with her. "I will," she responds when they end with, "You have to keep the faith."

Maybe it was the break in the weather, the sudden burst of color, and the swelling sonata the crickets broke into just as he stepped onto the front porch that morning. Maybe it was all of those things as well as the four martinis he'd had after work, but he came to her that night, kissing her gently on the back of her neck, stirring her from her sleep.

It had been seven months.

His hand reached beneath her nightgown; while his mind reminded him, "Just touch below the waist, only below the waist."

The amber-colored medicine bottles on the nightstand seemed to mock him beneath the moonlight and he climbed over her, so that his back was to the window, his face flush with hers. She was smiling, but her eyes were crying. He didn't want to see that, didn't want her hand gently tracing the outline of his jaw, her lips trembling and the grateful tone in her voice when she uttered "Bryant, oh God, Bryant."

He was a bad husband, a piece of shit of a man. She should be slapping him, he thought to himself.

He kissed her roughly on the mouth. Camilla felt her breath catch in her throat. Their teeth collided and then Camilla remembered to open her mouth. His tongue was urgent, his hands gripped and pulled at the soft skin of her waist, clutched at the swell of her buttocks, pulling at the waistband of her panties.

It was habit. It was habit for her to want to be naked, to strip everything from her body. She helped him get her panties off and watched as they sailed through the darkness and landed somewhere on the floor. He had his finger up inside of her. Probing, searching for the wetness but there was none. Atrophy had set in just like the cancer literature had suggested it would. She was desert dry.

Camilla looked wildly around and spotted the tube of A&D ointment on the nightstand. Somehow, in the frenzy that was Bryant, she got hold of it, but not before sending the phone crashing to the ground.

He helped her. They squeezed the tube together and then smeared the golden gel around the place that would receive him.

It was habit, and the gown was already pushed up and around her waist, not far at all to go to total nakedness and distracted, drunk, nibbling at her belly, lost in the past.

Camilla did as she had done in the past; she reached down and lifted the hem of the gown up and over her head.

"No!" Bryant suddenly screamed and Camilla felt sure, his demand echoed the length of the block, but it was too late, the gown lay in a pile on the pillow, just above her head.

Bryant looked towards the window, his halting palm just inches from her face. "No, don't," he whispered.

His lips started to quiver and right there between her legs, he melted into the five-year-old boy that Babette had told her had gone green at the sight of his own blood.

"I'm sorry, I'm so sorry," he chanted, never once looking at her, his tears wetting her belly. "I'm so sorry."

They remained that way for a while. Camilla pulling a pillow over her scarred chest. Her own tears unable to spill, just a well-deep loneliness swelling inside of her.

Two weeks later, Bryant's cheeks were still flushed pink with embarrassment and Camilla swore her skin was scorched where he had touched her. The whole experience had been a painful one and so Margot's impending visit would be a welcomed distraction.

"Can't she catch a cab in?" follows Camilla's suggestion that Bryant collects Margot at the airport.

Camilla's right eye widens and the eyebrow she has drawn in place of the real one climbs absurdly onto her forehead. "Okay, jeez," he complains as he snatches up the car keys and starts out the door.

He catches sight of Margot just behind the Asian couple holding hands. She doesn't just walk down the Jetway. She bounces, like a ball. Lit, he's sure, from a half-dozen or so of the miniature bottles of vodka she's had on the plane.

She's smiling broadly, her face a bit flushed, and a new color on her lips, one he finds attractive. Camel-colored leather jacket flapping open as she comes, bosom jiggling beneath the thin aqua-colored blouse. Her denim skirt stops midthigh, boots, brown like the jacket, hug her calves, squeezing them so tight that the flesh pops out from over the tops.

She's a bit bowlegged. He'd never noticed that before.

She spots him and waves. He smiles and waves back.

Pocketbook, magazine. That's it. He supposes they'll be spending some time together at baggage claim.

"Bryant!" she sings and embraces him. He's covered in perfume, arms and then lips on both cheeks, before she breaks away to step back and admire him.

He has to resist the urge to pull her back.

"How are you?"

She's beaming. The picture of health. A sight for sore eyes.

"I'm fine," he says and then he can't control himself and steps forward and hugs her again.

He misses the feel of breasts pressed against him. He holds her a moment too long and feels a flame ignite in his loins.

"You look good," he says.

"Don't I always?" she teases and winks.

She begins to ramble as they follow the baggage claim/exit signs. Margot talks about things he could care less about, but he keeps the practiced look of interest on his face and tries not to look at them, her breasts, but he can't help it. Everybody else is looking, even the women, so Bryant steals glances and pretends that the turn of his head is for the magazine racks and kiosks that display silk scarves, music CD's and a variety of sunglasses.

Location C and the suitcases, small and large, mostly black; some have colorful ribbons tied to the handle and there is the occasional oversized name tag.

Margot talks on and on and Bryant does not hear a word, but nods his head and blinks at people that step into his view. He ponders, *I wonder if she will let me see them, touch them maybe?*

He shouldn't have to go to strangers, barmaids that whispered in his ear after four martinis, just how long they'd been admiring him, had a thing for, have wanted to fuck him.

Secretaries, administrative assistants, Peggy in accounting, suddenly wearing blouses with four buttons undone instead of two.

He'd never viewed himself as a cheat; but he was still alive, still a man — but with Camilla the way she was, looking the way she did, "Who could really blame you?" was how Babette had ended her discussion with him about discretion. He had bedded the daughter of a close family friend and the news had gotten back to Babette.

They rode in silence for a while as Margot checked her makeup in the visor mirror. She checked her teeth and then swatted playfully at his arm. "Why didn't you tell me I had lipstick on my teeth?" Bryant just shrugged as she rubbed her index finger vigorously across her front teeth.

"Okay," she started and sighed. "What should I prepare myself for?"

Bryant reached over and turned the radio on.

"Well, she's lost a little more weight and . . ." He trailed off. She waited, but he said nothing more.

"Well, I brought her some more wigs. Real classy ones. No one will be able to tell that it's not her hair."

Bryant nodded and hit the turn signal.

Margot reached over and squeezed his thigh. "I know it's been hard for you," she said and her hand lingered.

Bryant turned and looked at her.

"She's lucky to have you. You're such a good person. Such a good man," she said and then slid her hand up and down his thigh a few times, before giving it one last pat, pat, pat, and then moving her hand back to her lap.

He was a good man, a damn good man. But a man just the same.

He stared at Margot.

A car-horn blast sounded from the Ford Explorer behind him and Bryant turned the steering wheel left.

Smoky cognac-scented perfume embraces her and then Margot follows. Words bounce between them as Bryant takes the suitcases upstairs. "So much luggage for just three days?"

"I'm going to stay a week."

"Oh."

"You look good."

"So do you."

"I like that perfume."

"Paradise."

"Smells good."

"Where's my girl?"

"Napping."

Margot removes her jacket and flings it onto the sofa.

Camilla thinks that Margot's breasts look bigger. They seemed to fill the room. Camilla touched her throat; suddenly she found it hard to breathe. "You okay?" Margot's face twists with concern. "Fine." Camilla smiled.

Maybe they were so consuming because she was the only one in the room who had any.

A bottle of wine led to two, but Camilla only drinking water and snacking on cheese bits while Zola fussed and carried on in her lap. "She's overtired," Camilla said, yawning herself.

"Poor thing," Margot said, "she's had such a busy day."

Lena strolls through. She walks the same way all day, no matter how long she's been moving about or how lengthy or demanding the hours have been; her stride remains purposeful. "Miss Camilla, can I take Zola up for you?" she asks.

"No, no Lena. I can manage."

"Well, I'll just finish up in here," Lena says.

"No, Lena. Please, you've already done more than enough," Camilla says, noting the time. "Go on ahead and relax."

"Sure?"

"Yes," Camilla says and looks at Bryant for support.

"Yes," he agrees when he can't take

Camilla's gaze much longer. "And thank you."

"Isn't she supposed to do the cleaning up?" Margot utters and tips her wineglass to her lips.

There were still party streamers here and there and the *Happy 2nd Birthday Zola* banner that hung over the front door.

"I'm turning in," Camilla said and kissed a squirming, complaining Zola on her cheek. "And so are you, li'l miss sunshine."

Margot blew them both a kiss. "Sleep tight."

"Yeah." Bryant yawned.

They sat there, the two of them watching the flames curl the logs into ashes. Another bottle of wine was opened and poured and the conversation jumping from here to there and laughter that brought tears to their eyes and then her hand was on his thigh again, his eyes on her breasts again and suddenly the kiss that should have been a brotherly-sisterly type of thing found itself mixed up with lips and tongues and his hands moving everywhere and then to where they needed to be, where he'd wanted them to be from the first time he saw her.

He takes her on the kitchen counter. Things scatter, but the paper plates are practically soundless when they fall on terra-cotta tiles. She wants him between her legs, but he has to see her breasts first and rips at her blouse, tears at her bra and there they are, big and beautiful, nipples erect and ready for licking, primed for sucking and he does so until his tongue is numb and she moans and pushes his head away.

It's a game for her. She loves men and sex and all of the spoils that come in between and reaches over and grabs the whipped cream and sprays white sugar-sweet circles of cream around her nipples, dragging Bryant back to his summer wedding day and her in that godawful dress and too much makeup and he backs away from her, turns and snatches the cabinet door open and pulls out the dessert plates.

The guilt is immediate. The shame follows almost as quickly and they both, still panting and sweating and smelling of each other's funk, hurry to hide themselves from the other.

His manhood, still dripping, but shriveled now and not worthy at all of the "oohs and ahhh's" Margot let out on first sight, is hurriedly shoved back into his boxers. His pants are pulled up from around his ankles, zipped, clasped, belt latched.

Margot can't seem to get her bra hooked.

Her hands are shaking and she looks to Bryant for help but he's already in the dining room, clearing away reminders of the joyful day.

They don't speak to each other. Instead, the crystal wineglasses are set in the dishwasher in silence and the counter is wiped free of cake frosting, ketchup from some child's forgotten hot dog and them.

Margot heads up to bed, uttering good night as she goes.

Bryant nods his head without looking at her. Settling himself down onto the couch and waits for the second wave of guilt to wash over him, but it never comes and just before dawn, he climbs the stairs and goes to her again.

By Tuesday, he knows her likes and dislikes — his tongue down the center of her back, but not in her ears.

He'd never had a woman suck his fingers, but Margot has made him a lifelong fan of it now.

The hours that fall between midnight and dawn belong to them.

If it wasn't for the terrorist Camilla might not have ever known. She had missed the looks they exchanged over breakfast, the change in his walk and working hours, (A confident strut. No more late nights.) the puffiness around Margot's eyes and how she yawned her way through the days, even though she turned in every night just before nine.

"Maybe you're getting too much sleep?"

"Maybe."

Camilla had missed the private jokes they suddenly had between them and was foolish enough to feel appreciation toward Bryant when he began looking in on her every night around midnight, "You asleep, Camilla?" His whisper would filter through her dreams and find her six years old and lying on her back, Pooh bear resting on her belly and Poe to her left calling out the shapes the clouds made that floated above them and through a topaz-colored sky.

"Hmmm," is all she would be able to offer him, not wanting to let that part of her life go again.

"Sleep tight," he'd murmur before pecking her lightly on the cheek and pulling the door tightly shut behind him.

She missed all of the signs but then a plane smashed into one of the World Trade Center towers, a second plane into the other tower, another found itself lodged in a portion of the Pentagon, and still another went down in a field, and all Camilla could think to do was grab hold of Zola and go to her husband.

"Bryant," Camilla whispered his name as she adjusted Zola on her hip and slowly pushed the door of his room open.

He was taking a personal day so that he could take "My girls out to brunch and then maybe a movie," he'd announced over dinner. Camilla had liked the way he'd said "my girls" and it didn't bother her at all that he was including Margot. In fact, the two had giggled like grade-schoolers.

The room was dark except for the glow of the clock.

Bryant was meticulously neat and Camilla knew, even in the darkness, that she could walk toward the bed without ever having to worry about tripping over a stray shoe or discarded pair of pants.

She could make him out now, on the right side of the bed, a thin sheet twisted about his legs, bare chest rising and falling, his lips slightly parted.

Camilla rarely came in this room with its green-tea walls and nutmeg-colored carpeting, simply furnished, except for the grand four-poster bed.

Zola fussed on her hip and caught hold of

Camilla's scarf, pulling it free and exposing her bald head just as she bent over her husband's face and whispered his name. And just like years earlier, when Velma had stumbled upon Maggie and Lloyd in the root cellar, "What?" is what rolled off the tip of Camilla's tongue and dropped straight down into the pit of Bryant's ear.

This was Scotch Plains, and she was Camilla who had arrested her development and set out in search of normal, leaving behind the wisdom of her elders and figuring that she knew best, when she knew nothing at all as she stumbled her way along and right into life with all its beautiful imperfections. Because that's what life is, beautiful and imperfect.

And here was her sleeping husband who had sold her on something that had looked fresh and fine and normal and Camilla had said I love you and I will and I do, burying her yesterdays and guaranteeing her tomorrows — or so she thought.

Somehow fresh, fine, and normal had staled and spoiled and uglied up right there under Camilla's nose, in Camilla's house during the twilight hours when Camilla dreamed of Queens and Roses.

When the second plane hit, Camilla

found herself jerking backward, impacted by her own unbelievable turn of events. Her mouth spewed none of the other words that thrashed about in her mind, except for a lone and whispered, "What?" and then there was the snort that followed as she tried to clear her nose of the smoky cognac scent of Paradise.

Tuesday was their day.

There she is.

Standing in front of the place where she grew and bloomed and flourished. It'd been years, but the house still looked the same way she remembered it, except for the sun-shine-yellow paint, chipped and flaking off of the side and the car tires, spray-painted white and then fashioned into planters.

It is almost the same, that house, except the fence is new and radiant silver beneath a sun that is a little too brilliant for that September 12 day. Everything is almost as she remembers it, but those memories are marred by the mothers that weep and walk aimlessly up and down Rockaway Boulevard.

Camilla imagines there must be new sounds behind that front door with its new brass knocker. The children are grown and gone and the gutter has broken free from the house leaving a dark hiding space for squirrels and small brown birds.

She stands there on the sidewalk, where she once skipped rope and played jacks, red-light green-light, Mother may I and received, to some surprise, her first kiss.

Behind her, ticking sounds emanate from the cooling engine and Zola sleeps peacefully in her car seat.

Camilla stands there and wonders if she will be welcomed.

Did she really believe that they wouldn't even try to find her? With all of her book smarts she had no common sense at all, Velma had seethed.

Some people disappear off of the face of the earth. And some people climb into a cave and become hermits and then there was Camilla, who thought the change in the color of her skin made her invisible to those people who loved her.

It hadn't even taken much doing, a few phone calls and trip to Smith and a talk with a classmate and then another call to Bennington to verify the information.

If Camilla hadn't been in such a rush to leave, she would have known how small the world really was.

Parry Simmons, who had lived two doors

away from Velma for fifteen years, was now living in Plainfield, just a few towns away from Scotch Plains.

Her daughter Simone had got hold of a *Union County Times* paper and forgot it on the sofa table at the end of her visit. Parry, needing paper to wrap her trout in, flipped through it in search of coupons and found something much better, a picture of a woman looking suspiciously like Camilla, but calling herself Dear Rose.

Parry had clipped the column and the picture and mailed it along with a short note to Velma — she could have called, but she wasn't going to run up her long-distance bill for someone who she hadn't seen or spoken to in ten years.

Parry, being the woman that she is, then sent her own Dear Rose letter saying how much she enjoyed the column and if she could possibly be ". . . little Camilla from south Ozone Park, Queens?"

If Camilla thought they'd never lifted a finger to make sure that she was safe and sound and some sort of happy — then she was even more simpleminded than Maggie.

They knew about the wedding, some someone who had a friend that knew something or another passed word that the husband was "High, high yella!" and that "Camilla wasn't too far behind him in the complexion department." And "Does she have that skin condition that Michael Jackson has, just maybe?"

Velma grit her teeth. The only condition that Michael Jackson and Camilla shared, was the condition of having been born black. But she kept that thought to herself.

They went on and on, the people, about the amount of money Camilla's dress alone had cost. "Enough to feed a small African village," is the way the story had been told and all Velma could do was try not to feel angry as she walked through the muck of winter, her feet going numb against the icy slush that seeped through the thin soles of her boots.

And what about that time in Greenwich Village, did she think that Ivan hadn't recognized her?

He did. Pancake batter–colored skin and all — he knew it was her as soon as she turned the corner and so he had to shift his eyes and look distracted (for her benefit) and bite down on his tongue to keep from yelling out, "Milla, Milla, cuz where you been girl!" and shattering that mirror, mirror in her soul that had been telling her lies and getting it twisted for too damn long!

He kept quiet and let her have her exile; Lord knows he had had his.

But like yesterday, today they still cry for Doris who'd called from the ninety-eighth floor of the second tower, to say "I'm okay Grandma" and "Yeah, you're right some fool made a wrong turn" and "Well, they said there isn't a danger really, but I think I'm going to go on ahead and —"

That's when the second plane hit and the cameraman and the people on the street are just as surprised as Velma, Chuck, Audrey, and Maggie who clutched their hearts and leaned forward on the sofa in disbelief.

It took a moment before the four of them understood what had exactly happened. Velma looked into the white mouthpiece of the phone, pressed the receiver against her ear and whispered, "Doris?"

Maggie had placed her palms over her ears and began rocking in place. While all Chuck was able to do was shake his head and wipe at the tears that rolled swiftly down his face.

"Doris, *Dooooooorrrrrrrriiiissssss!*" Velma had screamed into the dead phone connection and then she was up, lightning-fast like someone had lit a fire under her behind, and she began sprinting back and forth between the kitchen and the front door.

Audrey wanted to catch hold of her mother, but she was too afraid to move, so she sat and watched, waited, and wished that she hadn't checked herself into rehab ninety-four days earlier.

She wished that she had waited some before she came back home and snuck up behind Velma — who was sweeping the front walk — and sputtered through the empty spaces of her teeth that "This time I'm clean for good, Mama, I swear."

She'd given a tired-looking Velma, who had heard that promise too many times before, the peace sign after she crossed her heart and swore to die.

It had not only sounded believable, it felt true. But what had gone on on the television, right before her very eyes, made Audrey wish that she had never kicked at all.

Velma's mouth was a large silent *O* as she streaked between rooms. No matter how fast she ran, the scream remained lodged in her chest until she collapsed to her knees and began beating it loose with her fists.

When it was finally freed, the house filled with sorrow just as the second building imploded.

Now Wednesday, the house quiet, but still very sad. Bobby called to say that he wouldn't be able to get to them for days.

He's married and living in California now, and has already loaded his family into his two-year-old minivan and started the cross-country trek.

Peggy, down in Florida, living with her second oldest child and taking care of her own grandkids, calls and checks and then proclaims, "I can't get on a plane, Mama, not ever again."

She'll take Amtrak in as soon as she can. Others call, check in, weep.

The only one who hasn't been heard from is Camilla who is standing and wondering on the sidewalk outside.

How her mind travels.

Streaking through time and space and settling on a joyful moment that Maggie could slip into and hide away from the pains of yesterday.

Maggie found a place last night with a nice patch of green that she recognized from her childhood before the confusing time when Velma stopped loving her. It was cool there and fresh-smelling and Maggie could feel her face smiling before Velma's weeping tore through the years and yanked her back to the very sadness she was trying to escape.

Now, morning time again and Maggie won't allow herself another day of endless hours in front of the television, reliving yesterday's horrors and so she settles herself in the chair next to her window, coaxing the old roller shade up and around its spindle; her eyes fall on a face that hasn't been seen in years.

Camilla sees the shade rise and then there is Maggie, eyes wide and seeing but not believing, Maggie wants to blink, but her eyelids won't even flutter and anyway, she thinks, maybe it's age, and even the good seeing eye don't see so well anymore and so she uses her hand to rub the good eye wet and clear and then finally she's able to blink and fully expects Camilla to be replaced with the bark of the tree or even a snowman, anything and anybody, because she has prayed and wished for Camilla's return and Audrey was the only part of her that kept coming back and so Maggie convinced herself that God was dead and only wishes of beautiful people came true.

Camilla waves. It's a little two-finger

wave that is brought on by shame and guilt and if she'd known about Doris, she wouldn't have offered the bright cheery smile she thought appropriate for the moment.

Maggie turns and looks at her wall and then the bed; unmade and the slippers, dozens of them, bottoms gone, filthy and lined up along the wall. Velma has tried to convince her to toss them away, but Maggie won't let them go, they represent the years she's been without Lloyd.

She looks at all of these things and wants to yell out for someone else to come and look and see if Camilla is who is standing out on the sidewalk waving at her.

Maggie shuffles into the living room and wants to say what it is she thinks she's seen, but the timing doesn't seem right. Velma's face is buried in Chuck's chest, her legs are folded beneath her on the couch, his hands gently stroke her hair and his eyes are wet and Maggie can see that Chuck is all the man that Velma has ever needed.

This is not the right time, especially if she's hallucinating and so Maggie makes a decision, turns and heads toward the front door.

★ ★ ★

Camilla balances Zola on her hip now. She thinks about the three suitcases that sit in the trunk of her car and how she doesn't even remember packing them or any of the many words she used to say good-bye, go to hell, and good riddance!

Just the bewildered look on Bryant's face and the shifting of the curtain in the window of the guest bedroom as Camilla guided the Audi out of the driveway.

All day and into the night she drives, not knowing where to go and remembering only after she's going north on the New Jersey Turnpike for the eighth time just as dawn begins to break, that *roots* are what sustains everything, whether green-stemmed and packed in dirt or flesh-toned and walking and so Camilla veers right and takes the exit that says New York-Holland Tunnel and heads toward home.

And now, Maggie peers through the spotted glass of the storm door and there is not a wrinkle on that familiar face; Camilla thinks and then she's suddenly twelve years old again and can't find the proper pose, undecided as to whether she should look or look away. A nervous tic takes hold of her smile and the lid of her right eye.

Too late to flee, so she stands awkwardly and waits.

Maggie's heart is quivering in her chest and she can feel her hands trembling at her sides. The ground is like an ocean and the trees swim around her as she battles with her fears. Clenching her eye tightly shut, she covers the last few feet in darkness.

Closer, Maggie can smell them; soft baby scents mixed with anguish and fear. Maggie stretches her hands out and touches a small face, a shoulder, salty wet lips.

Camilla grabs hold of Maggie's hand and kisses the rough palm. All of her apologies spill out in that kiss and Maggie's chest heaves and her eye flutters open. "Am I dreaming?"

Camilla can't speak so she shakes her head *no*.

"This one yours?" Maggie asks. Her eye never letting go of Camilla, even as she takes Zola into her arms. She can't help but stare at the sallow cheeks, the coffee-colored halos around her eyes, the skin that is more taupe than brown.

Camilla shakes her head *yes*.

"Collard greens good where you been, huh?"

Another nod and a smile.

Maggie starts toward the house, Camilla follows.

Like everywhere else in the world on that day, there will be weeping.

But in that house, joy will sit alongside sadness as they gather around the table and unravel the years in words, tears, and touch.

The *why* will be posed, set out, examined, and then put away for another time when they don't have to deal with the planning that comes along with death.

The moment is now, the question is coming and the beginning of forever commences:

"Long time since we had a baby in the house," Maggie cooed and looked down into Zola's smiling face. "Can you say *Maagee?*"

Acknowledgments

Heartfelt gratitude to my higher power, muse, guides, family, and friends.

Much appreciation to Dutton, my fabulous editor, Laurie Chittenden and equally fabulous agent, James Vines.

Cedric Smith, thank you for an outstanding cover!

Ms. Anita Abbott and family who look after R'yane and me like we were one of their own.

My fans.

Peace, light & love,

Bernice

About the Author

Bernice L. McFadden is the author of four national bestsellers, all published by Dutton: *Sugar*, *The Warmest December*, *This Bitter Earth*, and most recently *Loving Donovan*. Shortlisted for the Hurston/Wright Foundation Legacy Award and winner of two Black Writers Alliance Gold Pen Awards as well as an Honor Award from the American Library Association, McFadden lives in Brooklyn, New York.